PENGUIN BOOKS

The Friend of Madame Maigret

Georges Joseph Christian Simenon was born on 12 February 1903 in Liège, Belgium. He began work as a reporter for a local newspaper at the age of sixteen, and at nineteen he moved to Paris to embark on a career as a novelist. He started by writing pulp-fiction novels and novellas published, under various pseudonyms, from 1923 onwards. He went on to write seventy-five Maigret novels and twenty-eight Maigret short stories. Although Simenon is best known in Britain as the writer of the Maigret books, his prolific output of over 400 novels made him a household name and institution in Continental Europe, where much of his work is constantly in print. The dark realism of Simenon's books has lent them naturally to screen adaptation. Simenon died in 1989 in Lausanne, Switzerland, where he had lived for the latter part of his life.

GEORGES SIMENON

The Friend of
Madame Maigret

Translated by Helen Sebba

PENGUIN BOOKS

PENGUIN BOOKS

Published by the Penguin Group
Penguin Books Ltd, 80 Strand, London WC2R ORL, England
Penguin Group (USA) Inc., 375 Hudson Street, New York, New York 10014, USA
Penguin Group (Canada), 90 Eglinton Avenue East, Suite 700,
Toronto, Ontario, Canada M4P 2Y3
(a division of Pearson Penguin Canada Inc.)
Penguin Ireland, 25 St Stephen's Green, Dublin 2, Ireland
(a division of Penguin Books Ltd)
Penguin Group (Australia), 250 Camberwell Road, Camberwell, Victoria 3124,
Australia (a division of Pearson Australia Group Pty Ltd)
Penguin Books India Pvt Ltd, 11 Community Centre,
Panchsheel Park, New Delhi – 110 017, India
Penguin Group (NZ), cnr Airborne and Rosedale Roads, Albany,
Auckland 1310, New Zealand (a division of Pearson New Zealand Ltd)
Penguin Books (South Africa) (Pty) Ltd, 24 Sturdee Avenue,
Rosebank, Johannesburg 2196, South Africa

Penguin Books Ltd, Registered Offices: 80 Strand, London WC2R ORL, England

www.penguin.com

First published as *L'amie de Madame Maigret* 1950
This translation first published by Hamish Hamilton 1960
Reissued, with minor revisions, in Penguin Classics 2003
Published as a Penguin Red Classic 2006

2

Copyright © Georges Simenon Ltd, 1952
Translation copyright © Georges Simenon Ltd, 1960, 1967

Set in 9.75/13.25 pt Trump Medieval
Typeset by Rowland Phototypesetting Ltd, Bury St Edmunds, Suffolk
Printed in England by Clays Ltd, St Ives plc

ISBN-13: 978-0-141-02960-3
ISBN-10: 0-141-02960-9

Chapter One

The chicken was on the stove, a fine red carrot, a big onion and a bunch of parsley, with the stems sticking out, surrounding it. Madame Maigret bent over to make sure there was no risk of the gas, which she had turned down as low as possible, going out. Then she closed the windows, except for the one in the bedroom, checked that she hadn't forgotten anything, glanced at the mirror and, satisfied, left the flat, locked the door and put the key in her purse.

It was a little after ten o'clock on a morning in March. The air was crisp, with sparkling sunshine over Paris. By walking as far as the Place de la République she could have taken a bus going right to the Boulevard Barbès and reached the Place d'Anvers in plenty of time for her eleven o'clock appointment.

On account of the young lady, she went down the stairs to the Richard-Lenoir métro station, just a step or two from her own door, and made the whole journey underground, looking vaguely, at every stop, at the familiar posters on the cream-coloured walls.

Maigret had made fun of her, though not too much, for he had had a lot on his mind the last three weeks.

'Are you sure there isn't a good dentist nearer home?'

Madame Maigret had never had any trouble with her teeth. Madame Roblin, the neighbour on the fourth floor – the lady with the dog – had spoken so highly of Dr Floresco that she had decided to go and see him.

'He has the fingers of a pianist. You won't even know he's working in your mouth. And if you're recommended by me he'll only charge you half the usual fee.'

He was a Romanian who had his surgery on the third floor of a building on the corner of the Rue Turgot and the Avenue Trudaine, exactly opposite the Place d'Anvers. Was this Madame Maigret's seventh or eighth visit? She had a regular appointment at eleven o'clock. It had become a routine.

The first time, she had arrived a good quarter of an hour early, thanks to her morbid fear of keeping anyone waiting, and had twiddled her thumbs in a room overheated by a gas fire. On her second visit she had also had to wait. Both times she had not been admitted to the dentist's surgery until a quarter past eleven.

For her third appointment, since there was bright sunshine and the square opposite was twittering with birds, she had decided to sit down on a bench and wait until it was time. This was how she had made the acquaintance of the lady with the little boy.

By now the habit was so well established that she would deliberately leave early and take the métro in order to save time.

It was pleasant to see the lawn, buds already half-opened on the branches of the few trees outlined against the wall of the high school. Sitting in full sunshine on the bench, one could follow the traffic on the Boulevard Rochechouart, the green and white buses which looked like huge beasts and the taxis darting in and out.

There was the lady, in a blue coat and skirt, just as on the other mornings, with her little white hat which was so becoming to her and so spring-like. She shifted over to make more room for Madame Maigret, who had brought a bar of chocolate with her and held it out to the child.

'Say thank you, Charles.'

He was two, and the most striking thing about him was his big dark eyes with immense lashes which made him look like a girl. At first Madame Maigret had wondered whether he could talk, whether the syllables he uttered belonged to any language. Then she had realized, though she hadn't gone so far as to ask their nationality, that he and the lady were foreigners.

'To me March is always the most beautiful month in Paris, in spite of the showers,' Madame Maigret was saying. 'Some people prefer May or June, but March has so much more freshness.'

She would turn round from time to time to keep an eye on the dentist's windows, for from where she was sitting she could see the head of the patient who usually preceded her. He was a man of about fifty, rather unfriendly, who was in the process of having all his teeth out. She had become acquainted with him too. He had been born in Dunkirk, lived with his married daughter in this neighbourhood, but didn't like his son-in-law.

The little boy, equipped this morning with a small red bucket and spade, was playing with the gravel. He was always very clean, very well cared for.

'I think I'll only have to come twice more,' Madame Maigret sighed. 'According to what Dr Floresco told me, he's going to start on the last tooth today.'

The lady smiled as she listened. She spoke excellent French, with a trace of an accent which lent it charm. At six or seven minutes to eleven she was still smiling at the child, who was greatly taken aback at having thrown dust in his own face; then all of a sudden she seemed to stare at something in the Avenue Trudaine, appeared to hesitate, and stood up saying urgently:

3

'Will you watch him for a minute? I won't be long.'

For the moment Madame Maigret hadn't been too surprised. With her appointment in mind, she simply hoped the mother would be back in time, and from tact she did not turn round to see where she was going.

The little boy hadn't noticed anything. He was still squatting there, playing at filling his red bucket with pebbles, emptying it and indomitably starting all over again.

Madame Maigret wasn't wearing a watch. Her watch hadn't gone for years, and she never remembered to take it to the watchmaker. An old man came and sat down on the bench; he must have been a resident of the neighbourhood, for she had seen him before.

'Would you be kind enough to tell me the time, monsieur?'

He must not have had a watch either, because he only answered:

'About eleven o'clock.'

The head was no longer to be seen in the dentist's window. Madame Maigret was beginning to be anxious. She was ashamed to keep Dr Floresco waiting; he was so kind, so gentle, and his patience was unfailing.

She looked all around the square without seeing the young lady in the white hat. Had she suddenly been taken ill? Or had she seen someone she wanted to speak to?

A policeman was walking through the square, and Madame Maigret stood up to ask him the time. It really was eleven o'clock.

The lady still did not come back, and the minutes were going by. The child had looked up at the bench and seen that his mother was no longer there, but he hadn't seemed to mind.

If only Madame Maigret could get in touch with the dentist! She would merely have to cross the street and go up three flights of stairs. Now she felt tempted to ask the old gentleman to watch the little boy while she went up to explain to Dr Floresco, but she didn't like to and she remained standing up, looking around her with mounting impatience.

The second time she asked a passer-by the time, it was twenty past eleven. The old gentleman had gone. She was alone now on the bench. She had seen the patient who preceded her come out of the building on the corner and walk off in the direction of the Rue Rochechouart.

What should she do? Had something happened to the nice lady? If she had been knocked down by a car she would have seen a crowd, people running. Wouldn't the child perhaps start getting upset now?

It was a ridiculous situation. Maigret would make fun of her again. It would be best not to mention it to him. She would telephone the dentist in a little while and apologize. Would she dare to tell him what had happened?

Suddenly she felt hot because her tenseness was making her blood tingle.

'What's your name?' she asked the child.

But he just looked at her out of his dark eyes without answering.

'Do you know where you live?'

He wasn't listening to her. It had already occurred to Madame Maigret that he might not understand French.

'Excuse me, monsieur. Could you tell me the time please?'

'Twenty-two minutes to twelve, madame.'

There was no sign of the mother. At noon, when whistles blew in the vicinity and a nearby bar was invaded by bricklayers, she still hadn't returned.

Dr Floresco came out of the building and got behind the wheel of a small black car, yet she did not dare leave the child to go and apologize.

What was worrying her now was her chicken, still cooking

on the stove. Maigret had told her that he would more than likely be home to lunch at about one.

Ought she to inform the police? In any case to do so she would have to leave the square. If she took the child with her and the mother came back in the meantime she would be out of her mind with anxiety. Goodness knows where she would run off to then or where they would finally catch up with each other! But she couldn't leave a two-year-old baby alone in the middle of a square either, just a step or two from the buses and cars which were passing in a steady stream.

'Excuse me, monsieur. Would you tell me what time it is?'

'Half past twelve.'

The chicken was certainly beginning to burn; Maigret would be coming in. It would be the first time in all these years of marriage that he wouldn't find her at home.

It was impossible to telephone him, either, because she would have to leave the square, go into a bar. If only she could see that policeman who had gone past, or any policeman, she would tell him who she was and ask him to be kind enough to ring up her husband. As if it had been deliberately arranged, there wasn't one in sight. She looked in all directions, sat down, stood up again, kept thinking she saw the white hat, but it was never the one she was waiting for.

She counted more than twenty white hats in half an hour, and four of them were worn by women in blue coats and skirts.

At eleven o'clock, while Madame Maigret was beginning to be worried, detained in the middle of the square by responsibility for a child whose name she didn't even know, Maigret was putting his hat on his head, leaving his office, addressing a few words to Lucas and walking glumly towards the little door which connects the offices of Police Headquarters with the Palais de Justice.

It had become a routine, dating from about the same time that Madame Maigret first went to see her dentist in the Ninth Arrondissement. The chief-inspector was entering the examining magistrates' corridor, where there were always some queer characters waiting on the benches, some of them between two policemen, and was knocking at the door that bore the name of Judge Dossin.

'Come in.'

In height Monsieur Dossin was the biggest magistrate in Paris and he always seemed to be embarrassed at being so tall, to be apologizing for having the aristocratic figure of a Russian wolfhound.

'Sit down, Maigret. Smoke your pipe. Have you read this morning's article?'

'I haven't seen the papers yet.'

The magistrate pushed one over to him with a big front page headline which read:

STEUVELS CASE
ME PHILIPPE LIOTARD APPEALS
TO THE LEAGUE FOR HUMAN RIGHTS

'I've had a long talk with the Public Prosecutor,' said Dossin. 'He agrees with me. We can't release the bookbinder. Even if we wanted to, Liotard himself would make some virulent attempt to stop us.'

A few weeks ago this name had been practically unknown at the Palais. Philippe Liotard, who was not much over thirty, had never pleaded an important case. After having been one of the assistants to a famous barrister for five years, he was just setting up on his own and still lived in a totally ordinary bachelor's apartment, in the Rue Bergère, next door to a house of ill-fame.

Ever since the Steuvels case had broken, he was mentioned

in the papers every day, gave sensational interviews, issued communiqués, even appeared on cinema screens in newsreels, his forelock belligerent and his smile sarcastic.

'Nothing new with you?'

'Nothing worth reporting, Monsieur le Juge.'

'Do you hope to find the man who handed in the telegram?'

'Torrence is at Concarneau. He's a resourceful chap.'

In the three weeks it had held public opinion in its grip, the Steuvels case had already run through a certain number of sub-titles, like a newspaper serial.

It had begun with:

THE CELLAR IN THE RUE DE TURENNE

By chance it happened that the setting was a district which Maigret knew well, which he even had a hankering to live in, less than fifty yards from the Place des Vosges.

Leaving the narrow Rue des Francs-Bourgeois, at the corner of the square, and following the Rue de Turenne towards the République, you come first, on the left, to a yellow-painted bistro, then to a dairy, the 'Crémerie Salmon'. Right next door is a glass-fronted workshop with a low ceiling and a dusty display case on which is written in tarnished letters: *Art Binding*. In the shop beyond, Madame Veuve Rancé runs an umbrella business.

Between the workshop and the umbrella shop-window is a large gate, under an archway, with the concierge's lodge to one side, and, at the end of the courtyard, an old town house, now riddled with offices and lodgings.

A BODY IN THE FURNACE?

What the public didn't know, what had been carefully kept from the Press, was that it was through sheer chance that the case had come to light. One morning, in the letter-box of Police

Headquarters, had been found a dirty slip of wrapping paper on which was written:

> *The bookbinder in the Rue de Turenne has burned a body in his furnace.*

It wasn't signed, of course. The paper had finished up on the desk of Maigret, who, sceptical, hadn't bothered one of his veteran inspectors with it, but had sent little Lapointe, a young man who was itching to distinguish himself.

Lapointe had discovered that there was indeed a bookbinder in the Rue de Turenne, a Fleming resident in France for more than twenty-five years, Frans Steuvels. Posing as a sanitary inspector, the detective had been through his premises and returned with a detailed plan.

'Steuvels works in the shop-window, so to speak, chief-inspector. The rear of the workshop, which gets darker as you move further away from the street, is cut off by a wooden partition behind which the Steuvelses have fixed up their bedroom.

'A staircase leads to the basement, where there is a kitchen, then a small room, where they have to keep the light on all day, which serves as a dining-room, and lastly a cellar.'

'With a furnace?'

'Yes. An old model which doesn't seem to be in very good shape.'

'Does it work?'

'It wasn't going this morning.'

It was Lucas who had gone to the Rue de Turenne at about five o'clock in the afternoon for an official investigation. Fortunately he had taken the precaution of bringing along a warrant, because the bookbinder claimed the inviolability of his home.

Detective Sergeant Lucas had been on the point of going away empty handed, and there were those who almost resented his partial success now that the case had turned into a nightmare for Police Headquarters.

Sifting the ashes at the very back of the furnace, he had come upon two teeth, two human teeth, which he had immediately taken to the laboratory.

'What kind of man is he, this bookbinder?' asked Maigret, who at this point was only remotely connected with the case.

'He must be about forty-five. He's red-haired, pock-marked, with blue eyes and a very gentle expression. His wife, although she's younger than he is, never takes her eyes off him as if he were a child.'

It was now known that Fernande, who had become famous in her turn, had come to Paris as a domestic servant and later had walked the pavement for several years along the Boulevard de Sébastopol.

She was thirty-six, had been living with Steuvels for ten years, and three years ago, for no apparent reason, they had been married at the Mairie of the Third Arrondissement.

The laboratory had sent in its report. The teeth were those of a man of about thirty, probably fairly fat, who must still have been alive until a few days before.

Steuvels had been brought into Maigret's office, amicably, and the grilling had begun. He had sat in the green plush armchair facing the window which overlooked the Seine, and that evening it was pouring with rain. Throughout the ten or twelve hours the interrogation had lasted, they had heard the rain beating against the window panes and the gurgling of water in the gutter. The bookbinder wore spectacles with thick lenses and steel rims. His abundant, rather long hair was shaggy, and his tie was crooked.

He was a cultured man, who had read a lot. He remained calm and deliberate; his delicate ruddy skin flushed easily.

'How do you explain the fact that human teeth have been found in your furnace?'

'I don't explain it.'

'You haven't lost any teeth recently? Nor your wife?'

'Neither of us. Mine are false.'

He had taken his plate out of his mouth, then put it back with a practised movement.

'Can you give me an account of how you spent the evenings of February 16, 17 and 18?'

The interrogation had taken place on the evening of the twenty-first, after the visits of Lapointe and Lucas to the Rue de Turenne.

'Do those dates include a Friday?'

'The sixteenth.'

'In that case I went to the Saint-Paul Cinema in the Rue Saint-Antoine, as I do every Friday.'

'With your wife?'

'Yes.'

'And the other two days?'

'It was at noon on the Saturday that Fernande left.'

'Where did she go?'

'To Concarneau.'

'Had the journey been planned long beforehand?'

'Her mother, who's a cripple, lives with her daughter and son-in-law at Concarneau. On Saturday morning we received a telegram from my wife's sister, Louise, saying that their mother was seriously ill, and Fernande took the first train.'

'Without telephoning?'

'They have no telephone.'

'Was the mother very bad?'

'She wasn't ill at all. The telegram didn't come from Louise.'

'Who did it come from then?'

'We don't know.'

'Have tricks of this kind ever been played on you before?'

'Never.'

'When did your wife get back?'

'On the Tuesday. She took advantage of being down there to spend a couple of days with her people.'

'What did you do all that time?'

'I worked.'

'One of the tenants states that dense smoke was coming out of your chimney all day on the Sunday.'

'That's possible. It was cold.'

This was true. The Sunday and Monday had been very cold days, and severe frost had been reported in the suburbs.

'What clothes were you wearing on Saturday evening?'

'The same as I'm wearing today.'

'Did anyone come to see you after you closed?'

'Nobody, except a customer who called for a book. Do you want his name and address?'

It was a well-known man, a member of the 'Hundred Bibliophiles'. Thanks to Liotard, more was to be heard of these men, who were nearly all important personalities.

'Your concierge, Madame Salazar, heard someone knock at your door that evening about nine o'clock. Several people were talking excitedly.'

'People talking on the pavement perhaps, but not inside my place. It's perfectly possible, if they were excited, as Madame Salazar claims, that they banged against the front.'

'How many suits do you own?'

'As I have only one body and one head, I own only one suit and one hat, apart from the old trousers and sweaters I wear for work.'

He had then been shown a navy blue suit found in the wardrobe in his bedroom.

'What about this one?'

'That doesn't belong to me.'

'How does this suit happen to have been found in your house?'

'I've never seen it. Anybody might have put it there in my absence. I've been here six hours already.'

'Will you try on the jacket, please?'

It fitted him.

'Do you see these stains which look like rust? It's blood, human blood, according to the experts. Unsuccessful attempts have been made to get rid of them.'

'I don't recognize those clothes.'

'Madame Rancé, the umbrella seller, states that she has often seen you wearing blue, especially on Fridays when you go to the pictures.'

'I did have another suit, which was blue, but I got rid of it more than two months ago.'

After this first interrogation Maigret was gloomy. He had had a long conversation with Judge Dossin, after which both of them had gone to see the public prosecutor.

It was the latter who had assumed responsibility for the arrest.

'The experts are in agreement, aren't they? The rest, Maigret, is up to you. Go ahead. We can't release that customer.'

By the next day, Maître Liotard had emerged from the shadows, and, ever since, Maigret had had him at his heels like a snapping mongrel.

Among the newspaper sub-headings there had been one that had had quite a success:

THE PHANTOM SUITCASE

Young Lapointe declared, in fact, that when he had looked around the premises, posing as a sanitary inspector, he had seen a reddish-brown suitcase under a table in the workshop.

'It was an ordinary cheap suitcase, and I knocked against it by mistake. I was surprised it hurt so much and I realized why when I tried to lift it, because it was unusually heavy.'

Yet at five in the afternoon, the time of the search by Lucas, the suitcase was no longer there. To be more precise, there was still a suitcase, also brown, also cheap, but Lapointe maintained that it was not the same one.

'That's the suitcase I took to Concarneau,' Fernande had said. 'We've never owned another one. We hardly travel at all.'

Lapointe was unshakeable, swore it was not the same suitcase, that the first one was lighter in colour, with its handle tied up with string.

'If I had had a suitcase to mend,' retorted Steuvels, 'I wouldn't have used string. Don't forget that I'm a bookbinder and a skilled leather-worker.'

Then Philippe Liotard had set off to collect testimonials from bibliophiles, and it had turned out that Steuvels was one of the best bookbinders in Paris, possibly the best, and that collectors entrusted their delicate work to him, especially the restoration of antique bindings.

Everybody agreed that he was an even-tempered man who spent practically his whole life in his workshop and the police were raking through his past to no avail in search of the slightest equivocal detail.

True, there was that episode in Fernande's career. He had known her when she was on the streets, and it was he who had taken her away from it all. But there was absolutely nothing against Fernande either, since that already long-distant period.

Torrence had been at Concarneau for four days. At the post office the original of the telegram had been found, printed by hand in block letters. The postmistress thought she remembered that it was a woman who had handed it across the counter, and Torrence was still searching, compiling a list of recent arrivals from Paris, questioning two hundred people a day.

'*We are fed up with the so-called infallibility of Chief-Inspector Maigret!*' Maître Liotard had declared to a journalist.

And he made reference to some trouble in a by-election in the Third Arrondissement which might well have induced certain people to precipitate a scandal in the district for political ends.

Judge Dossin, too, was getting it in the neck, and these attacks, not always discreet, made him blush.

'You haven't a single new clue?'

'I'm still looking. There are ten of us looking, sometimes more, and we're interrogating some people for the twentieth time. Lucas is hoping to find the tailor who made the blue suit.'

As always happens when a case arouses popular opinion, they were receiving hundreds of letters a day, almost all of which sent them off on false trails, causing them to waste a great deal of time. Nevertheless, everything was scrupulously checked, and even lunatics who claimed to know something were given a hearing.

At ten minutes to one Maigret got out of the bus on the corner of the Boulevard Voltaire and glancing up at his windows, as he always did, was a little surprised to see that the one in the dining-room was closed, in spite of the bright sun shining directly on it.

He walked heavily upstairs and turned the doorknob, which didn't yield. Occasionally, when Madame Maigret was dressing or undressing, she would lock the door. He opened it with his own key, found himself in a cloud of blue smoke and dashed into the kitchen to turn off the gas. In the casserole all that was left of the chicken, carrot and onion was a blackened crust.

He opened all the windows, and when Madame Maigret, all

out of breath, pushed open the door half an hour later she found him sitting there with a hunk of bread and a piece of cheese.

'What time is it?'

'Half past one,' he said calmly.

He had never seen her in such a state, her hat crooked, her lip quivering tremulously.

'Whatever you do, don't laugh.'

'I'm not laughing.'

'Don't scold me either. I couldn't help it and I'd like to have seen you in my position. And to think that you're reduced to eating a piece of cheese for lunch!'

'The dentist?'

'I haven't seen the dentist. Since a quarter to eleven I've been in the middle of the Place d'Anvers, without being able to move.'

'Were you taken ill?'

'Have I ever been taken ill in my life? No. It was on account of the baby. And in the end, when he began to cry and create a scene, there I was looking like a kidnapper.'

'What baby? A baby what?'

'I told you about the lady in blue and her child, but you never do listen to me. The one I met on the bench while I was waiting my turn at the dentist's. This morning she suddenly got up and went off, asking me to watch the child for a moment.'

'And she didn't come back? What did you do with the boy?'

'She finally did come back, just a quarter of an hour ago. I came home in a taxi.'

'What did she say when she came back?'

'To crown it all she didn't even speak to me. I was in the middle of the square, stuck there like a scarecrow, with the little boy yelling fit to draw a crowd.

'I finally saw a taxi stopping on the corner of the Avenue Trudaine and I recognized the white hat. She didn't even bother to get out. She half-opened the door, beckoned to me. The child was running ahead of me, and I was afraid he'd get run over. He reached the taxi first, and the door was closing again by the time I got there.

'"Tomorrow," she called. "I'll explain tomorrow. Forgive me..."

'She didn't thank me. The taxi was already going off in the direction of the Boulevard Rochechouart and it turned left towards Pigalle.'

She stopped, breathless, took off her hat with such a brusque movement that she rumpled her hair.

'Are you laughing?'

'Of course not.'

'You may as well admit that it makes you laugh. All the same she did leave her child in the charge of a stranger for more than two hours. She doesn't even know my name.'

'And you? Do you know hers?'

'No.'

'Do you know where she lives?'

'I don't know anything at all except that I missed my appointment, my lovely chicken is burnt, and you're eating a piece of cheese off a corner of the table like a . . . like a . . .'

Then, not able to find the word, she began to cry, making for the bedroom door in order to go and change her dress.

Chapter Two

Maigret had a manner all his own of climbing the two flights of stairs at the Quai des Orfèvres, his expression remaining pretty indifferent at first, at the foot of the staircase, where the light from outside struck it almost full strength, then growing more and more preoccupied the deeper he penetrated into the grey shadows of the old building, as though official worries thrust themselves more heavily upon him as he drew nearer to them.

By the time he passed the porter he was already the Chief. Recently he had got into the habit, both morning and afternoon, before pushing open his own door, of dropping into the inspectors' office and, his hat on his head, his overcoat on his back, going in to see the Grand Turenne.

This was the latest catchphrase at Headquarters, and it was indicative of the stature the Steuvels case had attained. Lucas, who had found himself left in charge of centralizing information, collating it and keeping it up to date, had quickly been swamped, for it was also his job to answer telephone calls, open all mail concerning the case and interview informants.

Incapable of working in the inspectors' office, where there was constant coming and going, he had taken refuge in an adjoining room on the door of which a facetious hand had before long written: *The Grand Turenne*.

As soon as a detective had finished an assignment, as soon as anyone came back from a job, a colleague would ask him:

'Are you free?'

'Yes.'

'Go in and see the Grand Turenne. He's recruiting!'

It was true. Little Lucas never had enough staff for all the checks he had to make, and there was probably nobody left in the department who hadn't been sent out at least once to the Rue de Turenne.

They all knew the crossroads, near the bookbinder's, with the three cafés: first the café-restaurant on the corner of the Rue des Francs-Bourgeois, then the 'Grand Turenne' opposite, and lastly, thirty yards off, at the corner of the Place des Vosges, the 'Tabac des Vosges', which the newspapermen had adopted as their headquarters.

For they were in on the case too. The detectives, for their part, took their drinks at the 'Grand Turenne' from the windows of which you could see the Flemish bookbinder's workshop. This was *their* headquarters, and Lucas's office had turned into a sort of local branch.

The most amazing thing was that good old Lucas, chained down by his classification work, was probably the only one who still hadn't set foot on the scene of action since his visit there the first day.

Nevertheless it was he who knew that corner better than any of them. He knew that after the 'Grand Turenne' (the café!) came a high-class wine merchant's, 'Les Caves de Bourgogne', and he was acquainted with its proprietors; he only needed to consult a card to find out what they had told every interrogator.

No. They hadn't seen anything. But on Saturday evenings they left for the Chevreuse valley where they would spend the weekend in a cottage they had built themselves.

After 'Les Caves de Bourgogne' came the shop of a cobbler named Monsieur Bousquet.

He, on the other hand, talked too much; only he had the

defect of not telling everybody the same thing. It depended on what time of day he was questioned, how many apéritifs and brandies he had gone to drink at one of the three cafés, he didn't care which.

Then came Frère's stationery shop, semi-wholesale, and at the rear, in the courtyard, there was a cardboard-making business.

Above Frans Steuvels's workshop, on the first floor of the former mansion, jewellery was mass-produced. This was the firm of Sass & Lapinsky, which employed about twenty girls and four or five men, the latter all with outlandish names.

Everybody had been questioned, some of them four or five times, by various inspectors, not to mention the numerous inquiries of the reporters. Two deal tables in Lucas's office were covered with papers, plans, memoranda, and he was the only man who could find his way around in the muddle.

And indefatigably Lucas went on bringing his notes up to date. Once more this afternoon Maigret came back to take up his position behind his back, not saying anything, pulling gently on his pipe.

A page headed 'Motives' was black with notes which had been crossed out one by one.

They had looked for a political angle. Not in the direction Maître Liotard had indicated because that wouldn't hold water. But Steuvels, who lived like a recluse, might have belonged to some subversive organization.

This hadn't led anywhere. The deeper they looked into his life, the more they realized that it was unexceptionable. The books in his library, examined one by one, were books selected from the works of the best writers of the whole world by an intelligent, unusually cultured man. Not only did he read and re-read them, but he made notes in the margins.

Jealousy? Fernande never went out without him except to do

her shopping in the neighbourhood, and from where he sat he could almost keep an eye on her in all the shops she patronized.

They had wondered if there might be a connection between the presumed murder and the proximity of Messrs Sass & Lapinsky. Nothing had been stolen from the jewellery manufacturers. Neither the owner nor the employees knew the bookbinder, except by sight behind his window.

Nothing from the Belgian angle either. Steuvels had left there at the age of eighteen and had never been back. He wasn't interested in politics, and there was no indication that he might belong to a Flemish extremist movement.

They had thought of everything. Lucas was accepting the craziest suggestions as a matter of duty; he would open the door of the inspectors' office and call one of them at random.

They knew what that meant. A new check to be made, in the Rue de Turenne or somewhere else.

'I may have got hold of something,' he said to Maigret this time, pouncing on a sheet of paper among the scattered files. 'I had a notice sent out to all taxi-drivers. One's just left here, a naturalized Russian. I'll get it checked.'

This was the word in vogue. *Check!*

'I wanted to find out whether any taxi had brought one person or more to the bookbinder's after dark on Saturday, February 17. The driver, by the name of Georges Peskine, was hailed by three people that Saturday at about quarter past eight near the Gare Saint-Lazare, and they told him to take them to the corner of the Rue de Turenne and the Rue des Francs-Bourgeois. So it was after half past eight when he dropped them, which doesn't fit too badly with the concierge's testimony about the noise she heard. The driver doesn't know who his fares were. But according to him the one who seemed the most important of the three, the one who spoke to him, was a Levantine.'

'What language were they speaking to each other?'

'French. One of the others, a big, fair, rather heavy man of around thirty, blessed with a strong Hungarian accent, seemed to be worried, uneasy. The third, a middle-aged Frenchman, not so well dressed as his companions, didn't seem quite up to them socially.

'When they got out of the cab the Levantine paid, and all three of them walked back up the Rue de Turenne towards the bookbinder's.'

If it hadn't been for this business of the taxi Maigret might never have thought of his wife's adventure.

'While you're working on the taxi-drivers you might just inquire about a little incident that happened this morning. It hasn't anything to do with our case, but it intrigues me.'

Lucas wasn't prepared to be so sure that it had nothing to do with his case, for he was ready to connect the remotest, most fortuitous events with it. First thing every morning he had all the metropolitan police reports sent up to him to make sure they didn't contain anything that might come within his field of activity.

All alone in his office he was coping with an enormous load of work, of which the public, reading the papers and following the Steuvels case like a serial, had not the least inkling.

Maigret briefly sketched the episode of the lady in the white hat and the little boy.

'You might also ring the Ninth Arrondissement police. The fact that she was on the same bench in the Place d'Anvers gardens every morning makes it seem likely that she lives in that neighbourhood. Let them check the whole area, the tradesmen, the hotels and boarding-houses.'

Check after check! In normal times you could sometimes find ten inspectors at a time smoking, preparing reports, reading newspapers or even playing cards in the next office. Now you hardly ever saw two together. Scarcely had they come in than the Grand Turenne would open the door of his den.

'Are you free, son? Come in here a minute.'

And one or more of them would set off on a trail.

The vanished suitcase had been hunted in the parcels offices of all the stations and in all the junk shops.

Little Lapointe may have been inexperienced, but he was a responsible young man, incapable of making up a story.

On the morning of February 21, therefore, there must have been in Steuvels's workshop a suitcase that was no longer there when Lucas went there at five o'clock.

Yet so far as the neighbours could recollect, Steuvels had not left home that day, and no one had seen Fernande go out with a suitcase or a package.

Had anyone come to collect any binding work? This had also been 'checked'. The Argentinian embassy had sent for a document for which Steuvels had created a sumptuous binding, but it was not bulky and the messenger had it under his arm when he left.

Martin, the most cultured man at Police Headquarters, had worked for almost a week in the bookbinder's shop, leafing through his books, studying the work he had turned out during the last few months, getting in touch with his customers by telephone.

'He's an amazing man,' was his conclusion. 'He has the most select clientele you can imagine. They all have complete confidence in him. What's more, he works for several embassies.'

But this angle yielded nothing mysterious either. If the embassies entrusted their work to him it was because he was a specialist in heraldry and owned the stamps for a large number of coats of arms, which enabled him to bind books or documents emblazoned with the emblems of various countries.

'You don't look happy, chief. But you'll see, something will emerge out of all this in the end.'

And good old Lucas, who never lost heart, pointed to the hundreds of sheets of paper he was blithely accumulating.

'We found some teeth in the furnace, didn't we? They didn't get there all by themselves. And someone handed in a telegram at Concarneau to lure Steuvels's wife down there. The blue suit hanging in the wardrobe had human bloodstains on it which someone had tried unsuccessfully to remove. Maître Liotard can talk and carry on until he's blue in the face; he won't budge me on that.'

But all this paper work, so intoxicating to the detective, weighed on the chief-inspector, who stared at it with a glaucous eye.

'What are you thinking about, chief?'

'Nothing, I'm wondering.'

'About releasing him?'

'No. That's the examining magistrate's business.'

'Otherwise you'd have him released, wouldn't you?'

'I don't know. I'm wondering whether to start the whole case over again from the beginning.'

'Just as you like,' replied Lucas, slightly offended.

'That doesn't prevent you from going ahead with your work, far from it. If we wait too long we'll never get it straight. It's always the same: once the Press interferes, everybody has something to say, and we're swamped.'

'All the same I've found the taxi-driver, just as I'm going to find Madame Maigret's.'

The chief-inspector filled a fresh pipe, opened the door. There wasn't a single detective in the next room. They had all gone off somewhere, busily occupied on the Fleming's case.

'Have you made up your mind?'

'I think so.'

He didn't even go into his own office, left the Quai des Orfèvres and immediately hailed a cab.

'Corner of the Rue de Turenne and the Rue des Francs-Bourgeois.'

Those words, which you kept hearing from morning to night, were becoming nauseating.

The residents of the neighbourhood, for their part, had never had such a time. All of them, one after the other, had had their names in the paper. Shopkeepers, workmen, all they had to do was to drop into the 'Grand Turenne' for a drink and they met the detectives, and if they went across the street to the 'Tabac des Vosges', which was famous for its white wine, they were greeted by the reporters.

Ten times, twenty times, they had been asked their opinion of Steuvels, of Fernande, and for details about their movements and behaviour.

Since there wasn't even a corpse, for certain, but merely two teeth, the whole thing was not at all tragic and it seemed rather like a game.

Maigret got out of the cab opposite the 'Grand Turenne', glanced inside, saw no one from Headquarters, walked a few steps and found himself in front of the bookbinder's workshop, where the shutters had been up and the door closed for the last three weeks. There was no bell, and he knocked, knowing that Fernande ought to be at home.

It was in the morning that she went out. Every day since the arrest of Frans, in fact, she would leave at ten o'clock, carrying three small casseroles which fitted onto one another and were held by a frame surmounted by a handle.

It was her husband's meal that she carried to the Santé Gaol in this way, by métro.

Maigret had to knock a second time and saw her emerge

from the staircase which connected the workshop with the basement. She recognized him, turned round to speak to someone out of sight and finally came to let him in.

She was in slippers and wore a check apron. Seeing her like this, a bit overweight, her face bare of make-up, no one would have recognized the woman who once walked the little streets adjoining the Boulevard de Sébastopol. She looked for all the world like a domesticated woman, a meticulous housewife, and in normal times she was probably a cheerful soul.

'Is it me you want to see?' she asked, not without a suggestion of weariness.

'Is anyone with you?'

She did not answer, and Maigret walked over to the stairs, went down a few steps, leaned over and frowned.

He had already been informed of the presence in the neighbourhood of Alfonsi, who liked to drink an apéritif with the journalists in the 'Tabac des Vosges', but avoided setting foot in the 'Grand Turenne'.

He was standing, very much at home, in the kitchen, where something was simmering on the stove, and even though he was slightly embarrassed he managed an ironical smile for the chief-inspector.

'What are you doing here?'

'You can see for yourself: paying a visit, like you. I have a right to, haven't I?'

Alfonsi had been attached to Police Headquarters but not in Maigret's department. For a few years he had been in the Vice Squad, where it had finally been made clear to him that in spite of all his political pull he was unwanted.

Short in stature, he wore very high heels to make himself taller, possibly with a pack of cards inside his shoes, as some people hinted, and he was always dressed with exaggerated elegance, a big diamond, genuine or paste, on his finger.

He had opened a private detective agency, in the Rue Notre-Dame-de-Lorette, of which he was both proprietor and sole employee, assisted only by a vague secretary who was primarily his mistress and with whom he was to be seen in the evenings in nightclubs.

When Maigret had been told of his presence in the Rue de Turenne, the chief-inspector had at first thought that the ex-detective was trying to pick up bits of information which he could later sell to newspapermen.

Then he had discovered that he was in the pay of Philippe Liotard.

It was the first time he had crossed his path in person, and he muttered:

'I'm waiting.'

'What are you waiting for?'

'For you to go.'

'That's too bad, because I'm not through yet.'

'Suit yourself.'

Maigret made as though to leave.

'What are you going to do?'

'Call one of my men and put a tail on you day and night. I have a right to do that, too.'

'All right! That's fine! No need to get nasty, Monsieur Maigret!'

He set off up the stairs, with an air of being quite at home in the underworld, winking at Fernande before he left.

'Does he come here often?' asked Maigret.

'This is the second time.'

'I advise you not to trust him.'

'I know. I know his type.'

Was this a discreet allusion to the days when she was at the mercy of the police in the Vice Squad?

'How's Steuvels?'

27

'All right. He reads all day long. He's confident.'

'And you?'

Was there really a hesitation?

'So am I.'

Nonetheless she was obviously rather weary.

'What books are you taking him now?'

'He's in the middle of re-reading Marcel Proust all the way through.'

'Have you read him too?'

'Yes.'

Steuvels had, in fact, educated the wife he had picked up long ago off the pavement.

'You mustn't think I've come to see you as an enemy. You know the situation as well as I do. I want to understand. At present, I don't understand. What about you?'

'I'm sure Frans hasn't committed any crime.'

'Do you love him?'

'That word doesn't mean anything. I'd need another word, a special one, which doesn't exist.'

He had gone up to the workshop again, where the book-binder's tools were laid out on the long table facing the window. The presses were at the back, in semi-darkness, and on the shelves books were waiting their turn among the work in progress.

'He had regular habits, didn't he? I'd like you to tell me as accurately as possible how he would spend a typical day.'

'Somebody else has asked me that already.'

'Who?'

'Maître Liotard.'

'Has it occurred to you that Maître Liotard's interests don't necessarily coincide with your own? He was unknown three weeks ago and what he is after is to get as much publicity for his own name as possible. It doesn't matter to him whether your husband is innocent or guilty.'

'Excuse me. If he proves his innocence, that will be a terrific boost for him and his reputation will be made.'

'And what if he obtains his release without having definitely proved his innocence? He'll make a name as a clever fellow. He'll be in great demand. They'll say of your husband:

' "Lucky for him Liotard got him off!"

'In other words, the guiltier Steuvels appears, the more credit Liotard will get. Do you realize that?'

'Frans realizes it, certainly.'

'Did he say so?'

'Yes.'

'Doesn't he like Liotard? Why did he choose him?'

'He didn't choose him. It was he who . . .'

'One moment. You've just said something important.'

'I know.'

'Did you do it on purpose?'

'Maybe. I'm sick of all this fuss about us and I realize where it's coming from. It doesn't seem to me that I'm doing Frans any harm by saying what I'm saying.'

'When Sergeant Lucas came to make his search on February 21 at about five o'clock he didn't leave alone, but took your husband along with him.'

'And you questioned him all night,' she said reproachfully.

'That's my job. At that time Steuvels still had no lawyer because he didn't know he was going to be charged. And since then he hasn't been released. He came back here only for a very short time, accompanied by detectives. Yet when I told him to choose a lawyer he named Maître Liotard without any hesitation.'

'I see what you mean.'

29

'So the lawyer saw Steuvels here *before* Sergeant Lucas did?'

'Yes.'

'Therefore it must have been in the afternoon of the twenty-first, between the visit of Lapointe and that of the sergeant?'

'Yes.'

'Were you present at the interview?'

'No, I was downstairs doing a thorough cleaning because I'd been away three days.'

'You don't know what they said to each other? They hadn't met before?'

'No.'

'It wasn't your husband who telephoned to ask him to come?'

'I'm almost sure it wasn't.'

Some children of the neighbourhood had their faces pressed against the window, and Maigret suggested:

'Wouldn't you rather we went downstairs?'

She led him through the kitchen, and they entered the little windowless room, which was very attractive, very cosy, with shelves of books all around, the table at which the couple had their meals and, in a corner, another table which served as a desk.

'You were asking me how my husband spent his time. He got up every day at six, winter and summer, and in winter the first thing he did was to go and stoke the furnace.'

'Why wasn't it lit on the twenty-first?'

'It wasn't cold enough. After a few freezing days the weather had turned mild again, and neither of us feels the cold much. In the kitchen I have the gas stove, which gives out enough heat, and there's another one in the studio that Frans uses for his glue and his tools.

'Before shaving he would go round to the baker's for croissants while I made the coffee, and we would have breakfast.

'Then he would wash and get to work straight away. I would

leave the house about nine, having finished most of my house-work, to do the shopping.'

'He never went out to deliver finished jobs?'

'Hardly ever. People would bring work to him and call for it. When he had to go out I used to go with him, because those were just about our only outings.

'We had lunch at half past twelve.'

'Would he go back to work at once?'

'Nearly always, after spending a few minutes in the doorway smoking a cigarette, because he didn't smoke while he was working.

'This would go on until seven o'clock, sometimes half past seven. I never knew what time we'd have dinner, because he always wanted to finish the job he was on. Then he would put up the shutters, wash his hands, and after dinner we would read, in this room, until ten or eleven o'clock.

'Except on Friday evenings, when we went to the Saint-Paul Cinema.'

'He didn't drink?'

'A glass of brandy every night after dinner. Just one little glass which would last him an hour, because he never took more than a sip at a time.'

'And on Sundays? Did you go to the country?'

'Never. He hated the country. We would loaf about all morning without getting dressed. He went in for carpentry a bit. He made these shelves himself and just about everything we have here. In the afternoons we'd go for a walk in the Francs-Bourgeois district or on the Île Saint-Louis, and we often had dinner at a little restaurant near the Pont-Neuf.'

'Is he stingy?'

She blushed and answered less spontaneously, with a question, as women do when they are embarrassed:

'Why do you ask me that?'

31

'He's been working like this for more than twenty years, hasn't he?'

'He's worked all his life. His mother was very poor. He had an unhappy childhood.'

'And yet he's supposed to be the most expensive bookbinder in Paris and he turns away more orders than he asks for.'

'That's true.'

'On what he earns you could live comfortably, with a modern flat and even a car.'

'What would be the point?'

'He claims that he's never had more than one suit at a time, and your wardrobe doesn't seem any more extensive.'

'I don't need anything. We eat well.'

'You can't spend more than a third of what he earns on living expenses.'

'I don't pay any attention to money matters.'

'Most men work for some special goal. Some want a house in the country, others have dreams of retiring, others do it for the sake of their children. He had no children, had he?'

'Unfortunately I can't have any.'

'And before your time?'

'No. He never knew any women, in a manner of speaking. He made do with you know what, and that's how I met him.'

'What does he do with his money?'

'I don't know. I expect he invests it.'

They had, in fact, discovered a bank account in Steuvels's name at the O Branch of the Société Générale, in the Rue Saint-Antoine. Nearly every week the bookbinder would deposit petty sums which corresponded to the amounts received from customers.

'He worked for the pleasure of working. He's a Fleming. I'm beginning to know what that means. He was capable of spending hours on a binding just for the joy of producing something out of the ordinary.'

It was odd: sometimes she would speak of him in the past tense, as if the walls of the Santé Gaol had already cut him off from the world, sometimes in the present, as if he would be home any minute.

'He kept in touch with his family, did he?'

'He never knew his father. He was brought up by an uncle, who placed him in a charity home when he was very young, which was lucky for him, because that's where he learned his trade. They were badly treated, and he doesn't like to talk about it.'

There was no exit from the flat except the workshop door. To reach the courtyard it was necessary to go out into the street and under the archway, past the concierge's lodge.

It was amazing, at the Quai des Orfèvres, to hear Lucas rattling off all these names, which Maigret could hardly keep straight, Madame Salazar the concierge, Mademoiselle Béguin, the fourth-floor tenant, the cobbler, the umbrella-shop keeper, the dairy woman and her maid; he talked about one and all as though he had always known them and could list their various idiosyncrasies.

'What are you preparing for him for tomorrow?'

'Ragout of lamb. He likes his food. Just now you seemed to be asking me what his chief interest is, apart from work. It's probably eating. And although he's sitting down all day and gets no fresh air nor exercise, I've never seen a man with such an appetite.'

'Before he met you had he any men friends?'

'I don't think so. He's never mentioned them.'

'Did he live here then?'

'Yes. He kept house for himself. Except that once a week

Madame Salazar would come and clean up properly. It may be because we don't need her any more that she's never liked me.'

'Do the neighbours know?'

'What I used to do? No; at least, not until Frans was arrested. It was the reporters who brought that up.'

'Are they cutting you?'

'Some of them. But Frans was so well liked that they're more inclined to be sorry for us.'

This was true on the whole. If a count had been made in the street of those for them and those against, the 'fors' would certainly have won.

But the residents of the neighbourhood didn't want it to be over too soon, any more than the newspaper readers did. The deeper the mystery, the more bitter the contest between Police Headquarters and Philippe Liotard, the more delighted people were.

'What did Alfonsi want you for?'

'He didn't have time to tell me. He'd just arrived when you came in. I don't like the way he comes in here as if it were a public place, with his hat on his head, saying *tu* to me and calling me by my Christian name. If Frans were here he'd have put him out long ago.'

'Is he jealous?'

'He doesn't like familiarities.'

'He loves you?'

'I think so.'

'Why?'

'I don't know. Perhaps because I love him.'

He didn't smile. He hadn't kept his hat on, as Alfonsi had. He wasn't being rough and he wasn't wearing his crafty expression either.

There in the basement, he really looked like a big man who is honestly trying to understand.

'Obviously you're not going to say anything that may be used against him.'

'Of course not. Anyhow, I have nothing of the sort to say.'

'And yet it's equally obvious that a man was killed in this basement.'

'The experts say so, and I'm not clever enough to contradict them. In any case it wasn't Frans.'

'It seems impossible that it could have happened without his knowledge.'

'I know what you're going to say, but I tell you again that he's innocent.'

Maigret stood up, sighing. He was glad she hadn't offered him a drink, as so many people feel obliged to do in such circumstances.

'I'm trying to start afresh at the beginning,' he admitted. 'My intention in coming here was to go over the scene again inch by inch.'

'Aren't you going to do so? They've turned everything upside down so many times!'

'I don't feel in the mood for it. I may come back. I expect I'll have some more questions to ask you.'

'You know that I tell Frans everything on visiting day?'

'Yes, I understand you.'

He started up the narrow stairs, and she followed him into the workshop, now almost dark, and opened the door for him. Both of them simultaneously noticed Alfonsi waiting at the corner of the street.

'Are you going to let him in?'

'I'm wondering. I'm tired.'

'Would you like me to tell him to leave you in peace?'

'For tonight in any case.'

'Goodnight.'

She said goodnight too, and he walked heavily towards the

former Vice Squad detective. When he came up to him, on the corner, two young reporters were watching them from the window of the 'Tabac des Vosges'.

'Buzz off!'

'Why?'

'Never mind. Because she doesn't want you bothering her again tonight. See?'

'Why are you so nasty to me?'

'Simply because I don't like your face.'

And turning his back on him, he conformed to tradition by going into the 'Grand Turenne' for a glass of beer.

Chapter Three

The sun was still shining brightly, and there was a nip in the air that caused a cloud of vapour at your lips and froze your fingertips. All the same, Maigret had decided to stand outside on the platform of the bus and he was alternately grunting and smiling in spite of himself as he read the morning paper.

He was early. It was barely half past eight by his watch when he entered the inspectors' office at the very moment when Janvier, perched on a table, was trying to get down, hiding the newspaper from which he had been reading aloud.

There were five or six of them in there, mostly the young ones; they were waiting for Lucas to give them their day's orders. They avoided looking at the chief-inspector, and some of them, casting a furtive glance at him, could hardly keep a straight face.

They had no way of knowing that the story had amused him just as much as it had them, and that it was simply to please them, because they expected it, that he was wearing his grumpy expression.

A headline was spread across three columns on the front page:

MME MAIGRET'S MISADVENTURE

The adventure experienced the previous day in the Place d'Anvers by the chief-inspector's wife was recounted down to the last detail, and the only thing lacking was a photograph of Madame Maigret herself with the little boy left on her hands in such a cavalier fashion.

He pushed open the door to call on Lucas, who had read the story too and had good reason to take the matter more seriously.

'I hope you didn't think I was responsible for it? I was thunderstruck this morning when I opened the paper. Honestly, I didn't talk to a single reporter. Just after our conversation yesterday I rang Lamballe, of the Ninth Arrondissement, and I had to tell him the story, but without mentioning your wife's name, when I asked him to try to find the taxi. By the way, he's just phoned to say that by sheer chance he's already found the driver. He's sending him over. The man will be here in a few minutes.'

'Was there anyone in your office when you rang Lamballe?'

'Probably. There's always somebody in here. And no doubt the door to the inspectors' office was open. But who? It frightens me to think that there might be a leak right here.'

'I suspected it yesterday. There was a leak as far back as February 21, because when you went to the Rue de Turenne to search the bookbinder's premises, Philippe Liotard had already been notified.'

'Who by?'

'I don't know. It can only be somebody in the building.'

'That's why the suitcase had disappeared by the time I got there.'

'More than likely.'

'In that case why didn't they dispose of the bloodstained suit too?'

'Perhaps they didn't think of it, or else they thought we wouldn't find out what kind of stains they were. Perhaps they didn't have time.'

'Do you want me to question the inspectors, chief?'

'I'll take care of it.'

Lucas had not finished going through his post, which was stacked up on the long table he was using as a desk.

'Nothing interesting?'

'I don't know yet. I'll have to check. Several tips about the suitcase, of course. An anonymous letter states simply that it hasn't left the Rue de Turenne and that we must be blind not to find it. Another claims that the root of the matter is at Concarneau. A five-page letter, closely written, reveals with supporting arguments that the government itself fabricated the whole business out of nothing at all in order to divert attention from the cost of living.'

Maigret went into his own office, took off his hat and coat, stoked right up, despite the mildness of the weather, the only coal stove still in existence at the Quai des Orfèvres, which he had had such a hard job to retain when central heating was installed.

Opening the inspectors' door a crack, he called in little Lapointe, who had just arrived.

'Sit down.'

He closed the door again carefully, told the young man once more to sit down and walked around him once or twice, glancing at him curiously.

'You're ambitious, aren't you?'

'Yes, chief-inspector. I'd like to have a career like yours. That's what you might call presumptuous, isn't it?'

'Are your parents well off?'

'No. My father's a bank clerk, at Meulan, and he had a hard time bringing us up decently, my sisters and myself.'

'Are you in love?'

He didn't blush, didn't seem embarrassed.

'No. Not yet. I still have time. I'm only twenty-four and I don't want to get married before I'm settled.'

'Do you live by yourself in a furnished room?'

'Fortunately not. My youngest sister, Germaine, is in Paris too. She works for a publisher on the Left Bank. We share a place, and at night she has time to cook for us, and that's a saving.'

'Has she a young man?'

'She's only eighteen.'

'The first time you went to the Rue de Turenne did you come straight back here?'

He suddenly blushed, hesitated a moment before replying.

'No,' he finally admitted. 'I was so proud and happy at having discovered something that I treated myself to a taxi and went around to the Rue du Bac to tell Germaine about it.'

'That's all, my boy. Thanks.'

Lapointe, uneasy, worried, was reluctant to leave.

'Why did you ask me that?'

'I'm the one who asks the questions, aren't I? Later on maybe you'll get a chance to do some interrogating too. You were in Sergeant Lucas's office yesterday when he telephoned the Ninth Arrondissement?'

'I was in the next office, and the door between them was open.'

'What time did you talk to your sister?'

'How do you know I did?'

'Answer me.'

'She stops work at five. She waited for me, as she often does, at the "Bar de la Grosse Horloge", and we had a drink together before going home.'

'Were you with her all evening?'

'She went to the pictures with a girl friend.'

'Did you see her girl friend?'

'No. But I know her.'

'That's all. You can go.'

He would have liked to offer a bit more explanation, but someone came to tell the chief-inspector that a taxi-driver was asking to see him. This was a big, red-faced man of around fifty who must have driven a hackney carriage in his younger days and who, to judge by his breath, had certainly swallowed several glasses of white wine for the good of his stomach before coming in.

'Inspector Lamballe told me to come and see you about the young lady.'

'How did he find out that it was you whose fare she was?'

'I'm usually in the rank in the Place Pigalle, and he came over for a word with me last night, the same as he had a word with all of us. It was me who picked her up.'

'What time? Where?'

'It must have been about one o'clock. I was finishing my lunch at a restaurant in the Rue Lepic. My cab was outside. I saw a couple leaving the hotel opposite, and the woman immediately made a dash for my taxi. She seemed to be disappointed when she saw the flag was down. Since I'd got as far as my liqueur, I stood up and called across the street to her to wait.'

'What was her companion like?'

'A fat little man, very well dressed, like a foreigner. Between forty and fifty, I can't say exactly. I didn't look at him much. He was turned towards her and was talking to her in a foreign language.'

'What language?'

'I don't know. I come from Pantin and I've never been able to tell one lingo from another.'

'What address did she give?'

'She was jumpy, impatient. She asked me to go to the Place

d'Anvers first and slow down. She was looking out of the window.

'Then she said, "Stop a minute and drive on again when I tell you."'

'She was beckoning to somebody. A motherly old soul was walking towards us with a little boy. The lady opened the door, pulled the kid in and ordered me to drive on.'

'Didn't it look to you like a kidnapping?'

'No, because she spoke to the lady. Not for long. Just a few words. And the lady seemed more relieved than anything else.'

'Where did you take the mother and child?'

'First to the Porte de Neuilly. There she changed her mind and asked me to drive to the Gare Saint-Lazare.'

'Did she get out there?'

'No. She stopped me in the Place Saint-Augustin. Due to the fact that I got caught in a traffic jam there, I saw her in my mirror hailing another cab, one of the Urbaine's, but I didn't have time to get its number.'

'Did you try to?'

'Out of habit. She was really in a state. And it was a bit queer, after taking me all the way to the Porte de Neuilly, to stop me on the Place Saint-Augustin just to get into another cab.'

'Did she talk to the child on the way?'

'A sentence or two, to keep him quiet. Is there a reward?'

'Maybe. I don't know yet.'

'You see, I've wasted my morning.'

Maigret handed him a note and a few minutes later was pushing open the door of the director of Police Headquarters, where the conference had begun. The department heads were there, grouped round the big mahogany desk, talking quietly about current cases.

'What about you, Maigret? And your Steuvels?'

From their smiles it was obvious that they had all read the

morning's story; once more, and again just to please them, he pretended to be disgruntled.

It was half past nine. The telephone rang, the director answered, handed the receiver to Maigret.

'Torrence wants to speak to you.'

Torrence's voice at the other end of the line was excited.

'Is that you, chief? You haven't found the lady in the white hat? The Paris paper's just arrived, and I've read the story. Well, the description fits someone I'm on the track of here.'

'Go on.'

'Since there's no way of getting anywhere with the fool of a postmistress here, who claims she can't remember a thing, I started a search in the hotels, the boarding-houses, questioning garage-men and railway station employees.'

'I know.'

'The season hasn't started yet, and most of the people arriving at Concarneau are local residents or people who are more or less familiar, commercial travellers and . . .'

'Make it short.'

For conversation had been broken off all around him.

'I was thinking that if someone had come from Paris or somewhere else in order to send off the telegram . . .'

'Yes, I see all that.'

'Well, there's a young lady in a blue suit and a white hat who arrived the very evening the telegram was sent off. She came in by the four o'clock train, and the message was handed in at a quarter to five.'

'Did she have any luggage?'

'No. Wait. She didn't stop at the hotel. Do you know the Hôtel du Chien Jaune down by the pier? She had dinner there and sat around in a corner of the café until eleven o'clock. In other words, she left again on the 11.40 train.'

'Have you verified that?'

'I haven't had time yet, but I'm certain of it because she left the café at exactly the right time, and she had asked for the railway timetable immediately after dinner.'

'Didn't she speak to anyone?'

'Only to the waitress. She read the whole time, even while she was eating.'

'Have you been able to find out what kind of book she was reading?'

'No. The waitress maintains that she had a foreign accent, but she doesn't know what it was. What shall I do?'

'Go back and see the postmistress, of course.'

'And after that?'

'Ring me or ring Lucas if I'm not in the office, then come back.'

'All right, chief. Do you think it's the same woman, too?'

When he hung up Maigret had a little spark of glee in his eye.

'Maybe Madame Maigret will have put us on the track,' he said. 'Will you excuse me, chief? I have some urgent checking to do myself.'

By chance Lapointe was still in the inspectors' office, visibly worried.

'You there, come with me!'

They took one of the taxis from the rank on the Quai, and young Lapointe still didn't feel any more confident, for it was the first time the chief-inspector had taken him out with him like this.

'Corner of the Place Blanche and the Rue Lepic.'

It was the time of day when, in Montmartre, and especially in the Rue Lepic, barrows were lined up along the pavements, piled high with vegetables and fruit fragrant with the smell of soil and springtime.

Maigret recognized on his left the little *table d'hôte* restaurant where the taxi-driver had had lunch and, opposite, the Hôtel Beauséjour, only the narrow doorway of which was visible between two shops, a delicatessen and a grocer's.

> *Rooms by the month, week or day. Running water. Central heating. Moderate charges.*

There was a glass door at the end of the corridor, then a staircase with a sign on the wall: *Office*. A hand drawn in black ink pointed upstairs.

The office was on the first floor, a narrow room facing the street, with keys hanging on a board.

'Anyone there?' he called.

The smell reminded him of the time when he was just about Lapointe's age, in the Hotels Section, and used to spend his days going from one boarding-house to another. It smelled of a mixture of washing and sweat, unmade beds, slop pails and food being warmed up on spirit lamps.

A slatternly woman with red hair leaned over the bannisters.

'What is it?'

Then, all at once, realizing that it was the police, she snapped crossly:

'I'm coming!'

She took her time upstairs, moving buckets and brooms; finally she appeared, buttoning her blouse over her protruding bosom. At close range, her hair proved to be almost white at the roots.

'What's the matter? They checked here only yesterday, and I have nothing but quiet tenants. You're not from the Hotels lot, are you?'

Without answering he described to her, so far as the taxi-driver's testimony permitted, the companion of the lady with the white hat.

'Do you know him?'

'I may. I'm not sure. What's his name?'

45

'That's just what I'd like to know.'

'Do you want to see my book?'

'First I want you to tell me whether you have a tenant who looks like him.'

'Nobody except Monsieur Levine.'

'Who's he?'

'I don't know. A very decent man, anyhow, who paid for a week in advance.'

'Is he still here?'

'No. He left yesterday.'

'Alone?'

'With the little boy, of course.'

'And the lady?'

'You mean the nurse?'

'Just a minute. Let's begin at the beginning so as to save time.'

'That'll suit me fine, because I haven't any to spare. What's Monsieur Levine done?'

'Just answer my questions, will you? When did he arrive?'

'Four days ago. You can check in my book. I told him I hadn't got a vacant room, and it was true. He insisted. I asked him how long for, and he told me he'd pay for a week in advance.'

'How could you accommodate him if you had no room?'

Maigret knew the answer, but he wanted to make her say it. In this kind of hotel the first-floor rooms are generally reserved for occasional couples coming in for a few minutes or an hour.

'There are always the "casuals'" rooms,' she replied, using the traditional term.

'Was the child with him?'

'Not at the time. He went to fetch him and came back with him an hour later. I asked him how he was going to manage with such a young child, and he told me that a nursemaid he knew would take care of him most of the day.'

'Did he show you his passport, his identity card?'

According to regulations, she ought to have asked for these documents, but she obviously hadn't complied.

'He filled out his slip himself. I saw at once that he was a respectable man. Are you going to make trouble for me just for that?'

'Not necessarily. How was the nurse dressed?'

'In a blue suit.'

'With a white hat?'

'Yes. She would come in the morning to bath the kid and then take him out.'

'And Monsieur Levine?'

'He would hang around in his room until eleven or twelve o'clock. I think he went back to bed. Then he would go out, and I wouldn't see him again all day.'

'Or the child?'

'Nor him either. Not much before seven o'clock at night. It was she who would bring him back and put him to bed. She would lie down on the bed fully dressed while she waited for Monsieur Levine to come home.'

'What time did he come in?'

'Not before one in the morning.'

'Would she leave then?'

'Yes.'

'You don't know where she lived?'

'No. I only know that she took a cab when she left, because I saw her.'

'Was she intimate with your tenant?'

'You mean did they sleep together? I'm not sure. From certain signs I think they did sometimes. They have a right to, haven't they?'

'What nationality did Monsieur Levine put on his slip?'

'French. He told me he'd been in France a long time and was naturalized.'

'Where did he come from?'

'I don't remember. Your Hotels man called for the slips yesterday, as usual on Tuesdays. From Bordeaux, if I'm not mistaken.'

'What happened yesterday at noon?'

'I don't know about noon.'

'During the morning then?'

'Someone called and asked for him about ten o'clock. The lady and the kid had been gone quite a while.'

'Who called?'

'I didn't ask him his name. An ordinary little man not very well dressed, a bit shabby.'

'French?'

'Certainly. I told him the room number.'

'He'd never been here before?'

'No one had ever called, except the nurse.'

'Did he have a southern accent?'

'More like a Paris accent. You know, the kind of man who stops you in the street trying to sell you fancy postcards or take you Lord knows where.'

'Did he stay long?'

'Well, he waited by himself while Monsieur Levine was getting ready to leave.'

'With his luggage?'

'How did you know? I was amazed to see him carrying his luggage out.'

'Did he have much?'

'Four suitcases.'

'Brown ones?'

'Nearly all suitcases are brown, aren't they? Anyhow, these were good quality, and at least two of them were real leather.'

'What did he say to you?'

'That he had to go away unexpectedly, that he'd be leaving Paris that day, but he'd be back in a little while for the child's things.'

'How much later did he come back?'

'About an hour. The lady was with him.'

'Weren't you surprised not to see the little boy?'

'So you know about that too?'

She was growing more cautious because she was beginning to suspect that the matter was of some importance, that the police knew more about it than Maigret wanted to tell her.

'All three of them stayed in the room quite a time and they were talking pretty loud.'

'As if they were quarrelling?'

'As if they were arguing at least.'

'In French?'

'No.'

'Did the Parisian take part in the conversation?'

'Not much. Anyhow, he went out first, and I didn't see him again. Then later Monsieur Levine and the lady left. As they passed me on their way out, he thanked me and told me he expected to be back in a few days.'

'Didn't it seem queer to you?'

'If you'd kept a hotel like this one for eighteen years, nothing would seem queer to you.'

'Did you clean up their room yourself afterwards?'

'I helped the maid.'

'You didn't find anything?'

'Cigarette ends all over the place. He smoked more than fifty a day. American cigarettes. Newspapers too. He bought just about all the papers published in Paris.'

'No foreign newspapers?'

'No. I thought of that.'

'So you were curious?'

'One always likes to know what's going on.'

'What else?'

'The usual rubbish, a broken comb, torn underclothes . . .'

'Any initials?'

'No. It was the kid's underclothes.'

'Good quality?'

'Pretty good, yes. Better than I'm used to seeing around here.'

'I'll be back to see you again.'

'What for?'

'Because some details that escape you at present will certainly come back to you when you think it over. You've always been on good terms with the police, haven't you? The Hotels Section doesn't bother you too much?'

'I get you. But I don't know any more.'

'Good morning.'

He and Lapointe were back on the sunny pavement in the midst of the bustle.

'A little drink?' suggested the chief-inspector.

'I don't drink.'

'You're quite right. Have you thought things over in the meantime?'

The young man realized that he wasn't talking about what they had just found out at the hotel.

'Yes.'

'Well?'

'I'll speak to her tonight.'

'Do you know who it is?'

'I have a friend who's a reporter on the same paper that printed that story this morning, but I didn't see him yesterday. Anyway, I never talk to him about what goes on at the Quai, and he often teases me about that.'

'Does your sister know him?'

'Yes. I didn't think they were going around together. If I tell my father, he'll make her go back to Meulan.'

'What's the reporter's name?'

'Bizard. Antoine Bizard. He's on his own in Paris too. His family lives in Corrèze. He's two years younger than me, and some of his articles carry his own by-line already.'

'Do you meet your sister at lunchtime?'

'It depends. When I'm free and not too far from the Rue du Bac I go to lunch with her in a snack-bar near her office.'

'Go and meet her today. Tell her what we found out this morning.'

'Should I really?'

'Yes.'

'What if she passes this on too?'

'She will pass it on.'

'Is that what you want her to do?'

'Go ahead. But be sure to be nice to her. Don't let it look as if you're suspicious of her.'

'But I can't have her going out with a young man. My father told me to be sure . . .'

'Go on.'

Maigret walked down the Rue Notre-Dame-de-Lorette just for the pleasure of walking and took a taxi only at the Faubourg Montmartre after dropping into a bar for a glass of beer.

'Quai des Orfèvres.'

Then he changed his mind, rapped on the glass.

'Go by way of the Rue de Turenne.'

He saw Steuvels's shop with its door shut, as it was every morning now, for Fernande must have been on her way to the Santé with her set of casseroles.

'Stop a minute.'

Janvier was at the bar of the 'Grand Turenne' and, recogniz-ing him, gave him a wink. What new check-up had Lucas assigned to him? He was deep in conversation with the cobbler and two plasterers in white overalls, and the milky tint of their Pernods was recognizable even at a distance.

'Turn left. Drive through the Place des Vosges and the Rue de Biragne.'

This meant passing the 'Tabac des Vosges', where Alfonsi was sitting alone at a little table near the window.

'Are you getting out?'

'Yes. Wait for me a minute.'

It was the 'Grand Turenne' he entered, after all, to have a word with Janvier.

'Alfonsi's across the street. Have you seen any newspapermen over there this morning?'

'Two or three.'

'Know them?'

'Not all.'

'Have you got much more to do?'

'Nothing very serious. And if you have anything else for me, I'm free. I just wanted to talk to the cobbler.'

They were a good distance away from the group and were speaking in lowered voices.

'Something occurred to me just now, after I read the story. The old chap talks far too much, you know. He's determined to be somebody and he'd make things up if necessary. Besides, every time he finds something to tell it means a few drinks for him. Seeing that he lives right opposite Steuvels's studio and works in his window too, I asked him whether any women ever came to see the bookbinder.'

'What did he answer?'

'Not much. He remembers one old lady in particular; she must be rich and she comes in a limousine with a chauffeur in livery who carries her books in. Also, about a month ago, a very elegant young lady in a mink coat. Wait! I made a point of finding out if she only called once. He says no, she came again a couple of weeks ago, in a blue suit with a white hat. It was a day when the weather was very fine, and the paper apparently carried an article on the chestnut tree in the Boulevard Saint-Germain.'

'We can trace that.'

'That's what I thought.'

'So she went down to the basement?'

'No. But I'm a bit suspicious. He's read the article too, that's obvious, and it's perfectly possible that he's making it all up just to get some attention. What do you want me to do?'

'Keep an eye on Alfonsi. Don't let him out of your sight all day. You're to make a list of the people he speaks to.'

'He mustn't know I'm tailing him?'

'It doesn't matter much if he does.'

'What if he speaks to me?'

'Answer him.'

Maigret went out with the smell of Pernod in his nostrils, and his cab dropped him at the Quai where he found Lucas in the middle of lunching off sandwiches. There were two glasses of beer on the desk, and the chief-inspector took one of them without compunction.

'Torrence has just phoned. The postmistress thinks she remembers a customer with a white hat, but she can't swear she's the one who handed in the telegram. According to Torrence, even if she were dead certain, she wouldn't say so.'

'Is he coming back?'

'He'll be in Paris tonight.'

'Call the Urbaine taxi company, will you? There's another cab to be traced, possibly two.'

Had Madame Maigret, who had a fresh appointment with her dentist, left early, as on the other days, in order to spend a few minutes on the bench in the Place d'Anvers garden?

Maigret didn't go home to the Boulevard Richard-Lenoir for lunch. Lucas's sandwiches looked tempting, and he had some sent up from the 'Brasserie Dauphine' for himself.

This was usually a good sign.

Chapter Four

Young Lapointe, red-eyed and scruffy like somebody who has slept on a bench in a third-class waiting-room, had given Maigret a look of such distress when the latter had entered the inspectors' office that the chief-inspector had immediately taken him into his own room.

'The whole story of the Hôtel Beauséjour's in the paper,' said the young man lugubriously.

'That's good! I'd have been disappointed if it hadn't been.'

Then Maigret had deliberately begun to talk to him as he would have talked to one of the old hands, to Lucas or Torrence, for instance.

'There are some people we know practically nothing about, not even whether they've really played any part in the case. There's a woman, a little boy, a rather stout man and another man who looks a bit seedy. Are they still in Paris? We don't know. If they are, they've probably split up. The woman only has to take off her white hat and get rid of the child and we can't recognize her any more. You see!'

'Yes, chief-inspector. I think I understand. But all the same I don't like to think that my sister saw that fellow again last night.'

'You can worry about your sister later. Right now you're working with me. This morning's newspaper story will alarm

55

them. There are two possibilities: either they'll lie low, if they've got somewhere to lie low, or they'll look for a safer hiding-place. In any case our only chance is if they do something to give themselves away.'

'Yes.'

Just at that point Judge Dossin telephoned to express his surprise at the newspaper's disclosures, and Maigret began to sum up the position again.

'Everybody's been alerted, Monsieur le Juge, the stations, the airports, the Hotels Section, the highway police. Moers, up in Criminal Records, is busy looking for photos which might correspond to our customers. We're questioning taxi-drivers and, in case the gang have a car, garage-men too.'

'Do you think this has some connection with the Steuvels case?'

'It's a lead, after so many others that haven't got us anywhere.'

'I'm having Steuvels brought up this morning at eleven. His lawyer will be here, as usual, because he won't let me exchange two words with him except in his presence.'

'Will you permit me to come up for a minute during your interrogation?'

'Liotard will protest, but come up anyway. Don't let it look as if we'd planned it.'

The curious thing was that Maigret had never met this Liotard, who had become, in the Press at all events, something like his special enemy.

This morning all the papers again carried the young lawyer's comments on the latest angles of the case.

> Maigret is a detective of the old school, of the period when the
> gentlemen of the Quai des Orfèvres could, if they chose, give a
> man the third degree until exhaustion drove him to make a

confession, keep him in their hands for weeks, pry shamelessly into people's private lives, in fact a period when any kind of trick was considered fair play.

He is the only person who doesn't realize that today tricks like these just don't go down with an informed public.

What is it all about, basically?

He has let himself be fooled by an anonymous letter, the work of a prankster. He has had an honest man locked up and has been incapable ever since of pinning any serious charge on him.

He won't give up. Rather than admit defeat, he is trying to gain time, playing to the gallery, calling Madame Maigret to the rescue, serving up to the public slices of cheap fiction.

Believe me, gentlemen, Maigret is out of date!

'Stay here with me, son,' the chief-inspector was saying to young Lapointe. 'Only, tonight, before you go home, ask me what you may tell your sister, won't you?'

'I'll never tell her anything again.'

'You'll tell her what I ask you to tell her.'

And from then on Lapointe acted as his aide-de-camp. That really meant what it said, for Police Headquarters was becoming more and more like a military base.

The office of Lucas, the 'Grand Turenne', represented the command post, to which runners made their way from all floors. Downstairs, in the Hotels Section, several men were busy going through registration forms in search of a Levine or anybody else who might be connected with the trio and the child.

The previous night, in most boarding-houses, the guests had had the unpleasant surprise of being awakened by the police, who had examined their identity documents; this had resulted in some fifty men and women whose papers were not in order spending the rest of the night at the Depot, where they were now queuing up for the identification parade.

In the railway stations travellers were being scrutinized without their knowing it, and two hours after the papers came out, the telephone calls began, soon becoming so numerous that Lucas had to detail an inspector for this job.

People had seen the little boy all over the place, in the most widely separated parts of Paris and the suburbs; some said, with the lady in the white hat, some, with the gentleman with the foreign accent.

Pedestrians would suddenly rush up to a policeman.

'Hurry! The child's at the corner of the street.'

Everything was checked, everything had to be checked if no chance was to be overlooked. Three detectives had gone out first thing to interrogate garage-men.

And all night long the men of the Society Section had been on the job too. Hadn't the manageress of the Beauséjour said that her visitor hardly ever came home before one o'clock.

It was a question of finding out if he was a regular patron of nightclubs, of interrogating barmen, dance hostesses.

Maigret, after attending the conference in the Chief's office, was prowling about the building, with Lapointe at his side most of the time, going down to the Hotels Section, up to Moers in Criminal Records, taking a telephone call here, a statement there.

It was just after ten o'clock when a driver from the Urbaine Company phoned. He hadn't rung up earlier because he had made a trip out of town, to Dreux, to take an old invalid lady who did not want to go by train.

It was he who had picked up the young lady and the little boy in the Place Saint-Augustin, he remembered it perfectly well.

'Where did you take them to?'

'The corner of the Rue Montmartre and the Grands Boule-vards.'

'Was there anyone waiting for them?'

'I didn't notice anyone.'

'You don't know which way they went?'

'I lost sight of them straight away in the crowd.'

There were several hotels in the vicinity.

'Ring the Hotels boys again!' said Maigret to Lapointe. 'Tell them to go over the sector around the Carrefour Montmartre with a fine comb. Do you realize now that if they don't lose their heads, if they don't budge, we haven't the remotest chance of finding them?'

Torrence, back from Concarneau, had gone for a stroll down the Rue de Turenne, to get back into the feel of it, as he said.

As for Janvier, he had sent in a report on his shadowing job and was still on Alfonsi's heels.

The latter had joined Philippe Liotard the night before in a restaurant on the Rue Richelieu, where they had had a good dinner, chatting quietly. Two women had joined them later, who bore no resemblance to the young lady in the white hat. One was the lawyer's secretary, a big blonde with the look of a film starlet. The other had left with Alfonsi.

They had both gone to the cinema, near the Opéra, then to a nightclub on the Rue Blanche where they had remained until two o'clock in the morning.

After which, the ex-detective had taken his companion to the hotel where he lived in the Rue de Douai.

Janvier had taken a room at the same hotel. He had just phoned:

'They're not up yet. I'm waiting.'

A little before eleven o'clock Lapointe, following Maigret, was to be introduced to a region of the Quai des Orfèvres which was unknown to him, on the ground floor. They had gone down a long deserted corridor, the windows of which overlooked the courtyard, and, reaching a corner, Maigret had made a sign to the young man to keep quiet.

A police van, passing under the entrance gate to the Depot, was entering the yard. Three or four policemen were waiting, smoking cigarettes. Two others got out of the Black Maria, from which they unloaded first a great brute of a man with a low forehead, handcuffs on his wrists. Maigret didn't know him. This one hadn't crossed his path.

Next came a fragile-looking old lady who might have been the chairwoman in a church, but whom he had arrested at least twenty times as a pickpocket. She followed her policeman like an old-timer, trotting along with little steps in her extra-wide skirts, knowing the right turnings to take to reach the examining magistrate's offices.

The sun was bright, the air steely blue in the patches of shade, with whiffs of springtime, a few newly hatched flies buzzing.

Frans Steuvels's red head appeared, bare of hat or cap; his suit was rather crumpled. He stopped, as though surprised by the sun, and one guessed that his eyes were half-closed behind his thick glasses.

He had been handcuffed, just like the brute: a regulation strictly enforced since several prisoners had escaped from this very yard, the latest of them by way of the corridors of the Palais de Justice.

With his hunched back, his flabby figure, Steuvels was typical of those intellectual craftsmen who read everything that comes their way and have no consuming interest outside their work.

One of the guards handed him a lighted cigarette, and he thanked him, took a few drags on it with satisfaction, filling his lungs with air and tobacco.

He must have been easy to handle, because they were treating him kindly, they gave him time to stretch his legs before taking him over to the building, and he for his part seemed not to bear his warders any ill-will, showed no rancour, no hysteria.

There was a slight basis of truth in Maître Liotard's interview. Normally Maigret himself would have followed his investigation through to the end before turning the man over to the examining magistrate.

If it had not been for the lawyer, who had appeared on the scene as soon as the first interrogation was over, Maigret would have seen Steuvels several more times, which would have given him a chance to study him.

He hardly knew him, having been alone with the bookbinder only for ten or twelve hours, at a time when he still knew nothing about him or about the case.

Rarely had he been confronted with a prisoner so calm, so much in control of himself, without there being any indication that this was an assumed attitude.

Steuvels would wait for the questions, head down, with an air of trying to understand, and he watched Maigret as he would have watched a lecturer developing complicated ideas.

Then he would take time to think, answer in a gentle, rather faint voice, in carefully chosen phrases, but without any trace of affectation.

He did not get impatient like most prisoners, and when the same question came up for the twentieth time he would reply in the same terms, with remarkable equanimity.

Maigret would have liked to get to know him better but for the last three weeks the man hadn't belonged to him any more but to Dossin, who would have him brought up, with his lawyer, twice a week on an average.

Fundamentally Steuvels must have been a shy man. The odd thing was that the judge was a shy man too. Noticing the initial

G. before his name, the chief-inspector had once made so bold as to ask him his Christian name, and the tall, distinguished magistrate had blushed.

'Don't tell anyone or they'll start calling me the Angel again, as my fellow students did at college and later in law school too. My Christian name is Gabriel!'

'Come on now,' Maigret was saying to Lapointe. 'I want you to go and sit in my office and take all messages while you're waiting for me.'

He did not go upstairs straight away, wandered about the corridors a bit, his pipe between his teeth, his hands in his pockets, like a man who feels at home, shaking a hand here, another there.

When he felt sure that the interrogation was under way, he went up to the examining magistrates' wing and knocked at Dossin's door.

'May I?'

'Come in, chief-inspector.'

A man had risen to his feet, small and slim, very slim, too deliberately well dressed, whom Maigret instantly recognized from having seen his photographs in the papers. He was young and put on a pompous manner in order to seem older, affecting a self-assurance which did not match his age.

Quite handsome, with a sallow complexion and black hair, he had long nostrils which quivered occasionally, and he would stare people in the eye as though determined to make them look away.

'Monsieur Maigret, I suppose?'

'None other, Maître Liotard.'

'If it's me you're looking for, I'll be glad to see you after the interrogation.'

Frans Steuvels, who had remained seated, facing the judge, was waiting. He had merely glanced at the chief-inspector, then at the police clerk at the end of the desk, who still had his pen in his hand.

'I'm not looking for you particularly. I'm looking for a chair, if you want to know.'

He picked one up by its back and straddled it, still smoking his pipe.

'Do you intend to stay here?'

'Unless Monsieur le Juge asks me to leave.'

'Do stay, Maigret.'

'I protest. If the interrogation is going to be conducted in these circumstances, I object strenuously, on the grounds that the presence of a member of the police in this office obviously tends to affect my client.'

Maigret refrained from muttering: 'Make your little song and dance!'

And he watched the young lawyer with an ironical expression. The latter was obviously not in earnest over a word he was saying. It was part of his system. In every interrogation so far he had precipitated incidents, for the most futile or extravagant reasons.

'There's no regulation to prevent an officer of Police Headquarters from being present at an interrogation. So if you don't mind, we'll go on where we left off.'

All the same Dossin was influenced by Maigret's presence and he took a little while to find his place in his notes.

'I was asking you, Steuvels, if you are in the habit of buying your clothes ready made or if you have a tailor.'

'It depends,' the prisoner replied after reflecting.

'On what?'

'I hardly bother about the way I dress at all. When I need a suit, I sometimes get it ready made, but I've also had them made for me.'

'By which tailor?'

'I had a suit cut several years ago by a neighbour, a Polish Jew, who has since disappeared. I think he went to America.'

'Was it a blue suit?'

'No. It was grey.'

'How long did you wear it?'

'Two or three years. I forget.'

'And your blue suit?'

'It must be ten years since I bought a blue suit.'

'But the neighbours saw you dressed in blue not so long ago.'

'They must have confused my suit with my overcoat.'

It was true that a navy blue overcoat had been found in the flat.

'When did you buy this overcoat?'

'Last winter.'

'Isn't it unlikely that you would buy a blue overcoat if your only suit was brown? The two colours don't match particularly well.'

'I don't try to be smart.'

All this time Maître Philippe Liotard was staring at Maigret with a look of defiance so intense that he seemed to be trying to hypnotize him. Then, just as he would have done in court to impress the jury, he shrugged his shoulders, a sarcastic smile on his lips.

'Why don't you admit that the suit found in the wardrobe belongs to you?'

'Because it doesn't.'

'How do you account for someone having managed to put it in that place, seeing that you practically never leave your house and your room can be reached only by going through the workshop?'

'I don't explain it.'

'Let's be reasonable, Monsieur Steuvels. I'm not trying to trap you. This is the third time at least that we've tackled this subject. According to you, somebody entered your home, unknown to you, to place two human teeth in the ashes of your furnace. Note that this person chose the day when your wife was absent and that in order to make sure she would be absent he had to go to Concarneau – or send an accomplice – to dispatch a telegram about her mother's illness. Wait! That's not all.

'Not only were you alone at home, which is hardly ever the case, but furthermore, that day and the following one, you had such a big fire going in the furnace that you had to carry the ashes out to the dustbins seven times.

'On this point we have the evidence of your concierge, Madame Salazar, who has no reason to lie and who is in a good position, in her lodge, to keep an eye on the comings and goings of her tenants. On Sunday morning you made five trips, each time with a big bucket full of ashes.

'She thought you had been doing some spring cleaning and burning old papers.

'We have more evidence, from Madame Béguin who lives on the top floor and who states that your chimney smoked incessantly all day Sunday. Black smoke, she specified. At one point she opened her window and noticed an unpleasant smell.'

'Isn't the old Béguin girl, who is sixty-eight, generally regarded in the neighbourhood as not quite all there?' the lawyer interrupted, crushing out his cigarette in the ashtray and taking another from a silver case. 'May I also point out that for four days, as the weather reports for February 15, 16, 17 and 18 prove, the temperature in Paris and its surroundings was abnormally low?'

'That doesn't explain the teeth. Nor does that explain the presence of the blue suit in the wardrobe or the bloodstains found on it.'

'You're making the charge and it's up to you to prove it. But

65

you're not even able to prove that the suit actually belongs to my client.'

'Might I ask a question, Monsieur le Juge?'

The magistrate turned to the lawyer, who had no time to protest, since Maigret, turning to face the Fleming, was already continuing:

'When did you first hear of Maître Philippe Liotard?'

The lawyer stood up to make a retort, and Maigret unperturbed, went on:

'When I finished questioning you on the night of your arrest, or rather in the early hours of the morning, and asked you if you wanted the services of a lawyer, you answered affirmatively and nominated Maître Liotard.'

'The prisoner has an absolute right to choose any lawyer he likes, and if this question is asked again I shall be obliged to bring the matter up before the Bar Council.'

'Bring it up then! Bring it up! It's you I'm talking to, Steuvels. You haven't answered me.

'It wouldn't have been at all surprising if you had mentioned the name of a famous barrister or lawyer, but that's not the case.

'In my office you didn't consult any directory, you didn't ask anybody any questions.

'Maître Liotard doesn't live in your neighbourhood. I believe that until three weeks ago his name had never appeared in the papers.'

'I protest!'

'Please do. As for you, Steuvels, tell me whether, on the morning of the twenty-first, before my detective's visit, you had ever heard of Maître Liotard. If you had, tell me when and where.'

'Don't answer.'

The Fleming hesitated, his back hunched, watching Maigret through his thick glasses.

'You refuse to answer? All right. I'll ask you something else. Did you receive a telephone call on that same day, the twenty-first, during the afternoon, concerning Maître Liotard?'

Frans Steuvels was still hesitating.

'Or, if you prefer it, did you ring anybody up? I'm going to take you back to the atmosphere of that day, which had begun just like any other day. The sun was shining, and it was very mild, so you hadn't lit your furnace. You were at work, facing your window, when my detective appeared and asked to inspect your premises on some pretext or other.'

'So you admit that!' interrupted Liotard.

'I admit it, Maître. It's not you I'm interrogating.

'You immediately realized that the police had their eye on you, Steuvels.

'At that time there was a brown suitcase in your workshop which was gone that evening when Inspector Lucas came with a search warrant.

'Who phoned you? Whom did you warn? Who came to see you between the visits of Lapointe and Lucas?

'I've had a check made of the list of people you ring up frequently, whose numbers you've written down on a pad. I checked your telephone directory myself. Liotard's name does not appear among those of your clients either.

'And yet he came to see you that day. Did you send for him or did someone you know send him to you?'

'I forbid you to answer.'

But the Fleming made a gesture of impatience.

'He came on his own.'

'You are referring to Maître Liotard, aren't you?'

Then the bookbinder looked at each of the men around him, and his eyes twinkled as if he took a certain personal delight in putting his lawyer in an embarrassing position.

'Yes, Maître Liotard.'

The latter turned to the police clerk, who was writing.

'You have no right to record these answers, which have nothing to do with the case. I did, in fact, go to see Steuvels, whose reputation was known to me, to ask him if he could do a binding job for me. Is that correct?'

'That's correct.'

Why on earth was a malicious little spark dancing in the bright pupils of the Fleming's eyes?

'It was actually about an *ex libris* with the family crest – yes, indeed, Monsieur Maigret, my grandfather was known as the Comte de Liotard and voluntarily stopped using his title when he lost all his money. So I wanted a family crest and came to Steuvels, whom I knew to be the best binder in Paris, though I had been told he was terribly busy.'

'You didn't talk to him about anything except your crest?'

'Pardon me. It seems that you are now interrogating me. Monsieur le Juge, this is your office, and I have no intention of being taken to task by a member of the police. Even when it was my client who was concerned I had serious objections. But for a member of the Bar . . .'

'Have you any other questions to put to Steuvels, chief-inspector?'

'No more, thank you.'

It was funny. It still seemed to him that the bookbinder was not annoyed at what had happened and that he was even looking at him with new found liking.

As for the lawyer, he was sitting down again, picking up a file in which he pretended to be absorbed.

'You'll find me in any time you want me, Maître Liotard. Do you know my office? The last but one on the left, at the end of the corridor.'

He smiled at Judge Dossin, who was not feeling very comfortable, and walked towards the little door that connects Police Headquarters with the Palais de Justice.

The place was more of a beehive than ever, telephones in use behind every door, people waiting at every corner, inspectors rushing up and down the corridors.

'I think there's someone waiting for you in your office, chief-inspector.'

When he pushed the door open, he found Fernande alone with young Lapointe, who, sitting in Maigret's place, was listening to her and taking notes. He stood up in some confusion. The bookbinder's wife was wearing a beige belted gabardine raincoat and a hat of the same stuff, without a trace of stylishness.

'How is he?' she asked. 'Have you just seen him? Is he still up there?'

'He's getting on very well. He admits that Liotard called at the studio on the afternoon of the twenty-first.'

'A more disturbing thing has just happened,' she said. 'Please, you must take what I'm about to tell you seriously. This morning I left the Rue de Turenne as usual to take his dinner to the Santé. You know the little enamel casseroles I put it in?

'I took the métro at the Saint-Paul station and changed at the Châtelet. I'd bought a paper on the way because I hadn't had time to read one.

'There was a seat near the door. I sat down in it and began the article – you know the one I mean.

'I had put the stack of casseroles on the floor beside me and I could feel the heat from them against my leg.

'There must have been a train due to leave because a few stations before Montparnasse a lot of people got into the carriage, a good many of them had suitcases.

'I was busy reading and not paying attention to what was

going on around me when I got the impression that someone was touching my casseroles.

'I just had time to see a hand trying to put the metal handle back in position.

'I stood up, turning to face the person next to me. We were pulling in to Montparnasse, where I had to change. Nearly everybody was getting out.

'I don't know how he did it, but he managed to upset the whole thing and make his way out on to the platform before I could see him full face.

'The food spilled all over the place. I've brought you the casseroles, which are practically empty, except for the bottom one.

'Look at them for yourself. A strip of metal with a handle on top holds the stack together.

'It can't open by itself.

'I'm sure somebody was following me and tried to slip some poison into the food meant for Frans.'

'Take it to the laboratory,' said Maigret to Lapointe.

'They may not find anything, because of course it was the top one they tried to put the poison in and it's empty. Can't you believe me just the same, chief-inspector? You must have realized that I've been honest with you.'

'Always?'

'As far as possible. This time Frans's life is at stake. They're trying to get rid of him, and those dirty crooks wanted to use me without my knowing it.'

Her bitterness was brimming over.

'If only I hadn't been so absorbed in my paper I might have had a good look at the man. The only thing I know is that he was wearing a raincoat just about the colour of mine, and that his black shoes were worn.'

'Young?'

'Not very young. Not old either. Middle-aged. Or rather a man of no particular age, if you know what I mean? There was a stain near the shoulder of his raincoat, I noticed it while he was getting away.'

'Tall? Thin?'

'Rather small. Average height at the most. Looked like a rat if you want my opinion.'

'And you're sure you've never seen him before?'

She thought for a moment.

'No. He doesn't suggest anything.'

Then, changing her mind:

'Now it's coming back to me. I was just reading the article with the story of the lady with the little boy at the Hôtel Beauséjour. He made me think of one of those two men, the one the manageress said looked like the type that sells fancy postcards. You're not laughing at me, are you?'

'No.'

'You don't think I'm making it all up?'

'No.'

'Do you think they were trying to kill him?'

'Possibly.'

'What are you going to do?'

'I don't know yet.'

Lapointe came back and said that the laboratory could not let them have a report for several hours.

'Do you think he'd better stick to prison food?'

'It would be safer.'

'He'll be wondering why I haven't sent him his meal. I won't see him till visiting hours in two days' time.'

She wasn't crying, wasn't making a fuss, but her dark eyes, deeply ringed, were full of anxiety and distress.

'Come with me.'

He winked at Lapointe, led her downstairs, through corridors which became more and more deserted the further they went. With some trouble he opened a little window overlooking the yard, where a police van was waiting.

'He'll be down in a minute. Will you excuse me? There's something I must attend to upstairs . . .'

He made a gesture towards the attic floor.

Incredulously she watched him, then took hold of the bars with both hands, trying to see as far as possible in the direction from which Steuvels was going to emerge.

Chapter Five

It was restful, after leaving the offices where the doors banged incessantly behind inspectors and where all the telephones were ringing simultaneously, to make one's way, up a permanently deserted staircase, to the attic floor of the Palais de Justice, where the laboratories and records were housed.

It was already nearly dark, and in the badly lighted staircase, which was like some hidden stairway in a castle, Maigret was preceded by his own gigantic shadow.

In a corner of an attic under the mansard roof, Moers, a green eyeshade on his forehead, his thick spectacles before his eyes, was working under a lamp which he would move closer to or further away from his work by pulling a wire.

This was someone who had not been to the Rue de Turenne to question the locals, nor to drink Pernods and white wine in one of the three bars. He had never shadowed anyone in the street, nor spent the night keeping watch outside a closed door.

He never got upset, didn't turn irritable, yet perhaps tomorrow morning would find him still hunched over his desk. Once he had even spent three consecutive days and nights at it.

Maigret, without saying a word, had drawn up a cane-bottomed chair, sat down near the inspector and lighted his pipe, on which he was puffing gently. Hearing a rhythmic sound on a skylight above his head, he realized that the weather had changed and it had begun to rain.

'Look at these, Chief,' Moers was saying, handing him, like a pack of cards, a stack of photographs.

It was a magnificent job he had turned out, alone in his corner. From the vague specifications that he had been given he had somehow brought to life, endowed with personality, three people of whom almost nothing was known: the fat, dark foreigner, with the elegant clothes: the young woman with the white hat, and finally the accomplice who 'looked like a man who sells fancy postcards'.

To achieve this he had at his disposal hundreds of thousands of record cards, but he was certainly the only person who carried enough of their data in his head to be capable of the job he had just patiently achieved.

The first batch, which Maigret was examining, contained around forty photographs of stout, well-groomed men, Greeks or Levantines in type, with sleek hair, rings on their fingers.

'I'm not too pleased with those,' sighed Moers, as if he had been faced with selecting the ideal cast for a film. 'You can give them a try anyhow. As far as I'm concerned, I like these better.'

There were only about fifteen photos in the second batch, and every one of them made one feel like applauding, they bore such a resemblance to one's mental picture of the person described by the manageress of the Beauséjour.

Turning them over, Maigret learned the profession of the subjects. Two or three were racecourse tipsters. There was a pickpocket who was especially familiar to him because he had personally arrested him on a bus, and an individual who hung around the doors of big hotels touting for certain specialized establishments.

A satisfied little spark was dancing in Moers's eyes.

'It's amusing, isn't it? I've hardly got anything on the woman, because our photos never show hats. But I'm keeping at it.'

Maigret, who had slipped the photographs into his pocket, stayed a few minutes longer just because he felt like it, then, with a sigh, went on to the laboratory next door, where they were still working on the food contained in Fernande's casseroles.

They hadn't found anything. Either the story was a complete fabrication for some purpose which he couldn't guess, or they hadn't had time to introduce the poison, or else it had been in the section that had all been spilled in the métro carriage.

Maigret avoided going back through the Headquarters offices and came out into the rain on the Quai des Orfèvres, turned up his coat collar, walked towards the Pont Saint-Michel and had to hail about ten taxis before one stopped.

'Place Blanche. Corner of the Rue Lepic.'

He felt out of sorts, dissatisfied with himself and with the way the case was going. He was particularly resentful of Philippe Liotard, who had forced him to abandon his usual methods and mobilize all the departments right at the start.

Now too many people whom he couldn't control personally were mixed up in the case, which seemed to be getting more and more complicated all by itself; new characters were appearing whom he knew almost nothing about and whose roles he couldn't even guess at.

On two occasions he had been tempted to go back to the very beginning of the inquiry, all on his own, slowly, deliberately, following his favourite method, but this was no longer possible, the machine was in motion, and there was no longer any way to stop it.

He would have liked, for instance, to question the concierge again, the cobbler across the street, the old maid on the fourth floor. But what was the use? Everybody had questioned them by now, inspectors, journalists, amateur detectives, people in the street. Their statements had been published in the papers, and they couldn't go back on them now. It was like a trail which has been heedlessly trampled on by fifty people.

'Do you think the bookbinder's a murderer, Monsieur Maigret?'

It was the driver, who had recognized him and was questioning him as if they were on familiar terms.

'I don't know.'

'If I were you I'd pay particular attention to the little boy. That seems to me the best lead, and I'm not saying that just because I have a kid his age.'

Even the taxi-drivers were taking part in it! He got out at the corner of the Rue Lepic and went into the bar on the corner for a drink. The rain was streaming in big drops from the awning around the terrace, where a few women were sitting as rigid as waxworks. He knew most of them. Some of them probably took their clients to the Hotel Beauséjour.

There was even one, a very fat woman, blocking the doorway of the hotel, and she smiled, thinking he wanted her, then recognized him and apologized.

He went up the badly lighted stairs, found the manageress in the office, dressed this time in black silk with gold-rimmed spectacles, her hair a flaming red.

'Please sit down. Will you excuse me a moment?

'A towel for Number 17, Emma!'

She came back.

'Have you found anything new?'

'I'd like you to examine these photos carefully.'

First he handed her the pictures of the handful of women Moers had picked out. She looked at them one by one, shaking her head every time, and passed the batch back to him.

'No. That's not the type at all. She's more refined than these women anyway. Perhaps not exactly refined. What I mean is "respectable". You know what I'm getting at? She looks like a decent little woman, whereas the ones you've shown me might be women who come to this hotel.'

'What about these?'

These were the dark-haired men. She still shook her head.

'No. That's not it at all. I don't know how to explain to you. These look too much like dagoes. Monsieur Levine, you know, could have stayed at a big hotel in the Champs-Élysées without being conspicuous.'

'And these?'

He handed her the last batch, sighing, and the moment she came to the third photograph she stiffened, cast a furtive little glance at the chief-inspector. Was she reluctant to speak out?

'Is that him?'

'It may be. Wait till I take it to the light.'

A girl was coming upstairs, with a client who kept to the darkest part of the staircase.

'Take Number 7, Clémence. The room's just been done.'

She shifted her spectacles on her nose.

'I'd swear it's him, yes. It's a pity he can't move. If I saw him walk, even from behind, I'd know him at once. But it's very unlikely that I'm mistaken.'

On the back of the photograph Moers had written a résumé of the man's career. Maigret noted with interest that he was probably a Belgian, like the bookbinder. *Probably*, for he was known under several different names, and his true identity had never been established.

'Thank you.'

'I hope you'll give me credit for this. I could very well have pretended not to recognize him. After all, they may be dangerous, and I'm taking a big risk.'

She reeked so strongly of scent, the odours in the house were so clinging that he was glad to be back on the pavement and to breathe the smell of the rain-washed streets.

It was not yet seven o'clock. Little Lapointe must have gone to meet his sister and tell her what had happened at the Quai in the course of the day, just as Maigret had advised him to.

He was a good boy, too easily upset as yet, too emotional, but they could probably make something of him. Lucas, in his office, was still acting as conductor of an orchestra, keeping in touch by telephone with all departments, all sections of Paris and anywhere else that the trio was being searched for.

As for Janvier, he was still sticking to Alfonsi, who had gone back to the Rue de Turenne and spent nearly an hour in the basement with Fernande.

The chief-inspector drank another glass of beer while he read the notes written by Moers, which reminded him of something.

> *Alfred Moss, Belgian Nationality (?). About 42.*
> *Music-hall artiste for about ten years. Member of*
> *an acrobatic team with parallel bars: Moss, Jeff*
> *and Joe.*

Maigret was remembering. He was remembering particularly the one man of the three who played the clown in baggy black clothes and interminable shoes, with a blue chin, a huge mouth and a green wig.

The man seemed completely disjointed, and after each leap he would pretend to fall so heavily that it seemed impossible he hadn't broken something.

> *Has worked in most countries of Europe and even in*
> *the United States, where he was with Barnum's circus*
> *for four years. Retired after an accident.*

Then followed the names by which he had been known to the police since then: Mosselaer, Van Vlanderen, Paterson, Smith,

Thomas ... He had been arrested successively in London, Manchester, Brussels, Amsterdam, and three or four times in Paris.

However, he had never been convicted, due to lack of proof. Whichever identity he was using, his papers were invariably in order, and he spoke four or five languages perfectly enough to change his nationality as he pleased.

The first time he had been prosecuted was in London, where he was claiming to be a Swiss citizen and working as an interpreter in a large hotel. A jewel case had disappeared from a suite which he had been seen leaving, but the owner of the jewels, an old American lady, testified that she herself had summoned him to the suite to translate a letter she had received from Germany.

In Amsterdam, four years later, he had been suspected of confidence tricking. No proof could be established, any more than it could the first time, and he disappeared from circulation for a while.

The General Investigations Department in Paris was the next to take an interest in him, again unsuccessfully, during a period when the cross-frontier traffic in gold was being carried on on a big scale, and when Moss, now Joseph Thomas, was shuttling between France and Belgium.

He had his ups and downs, living now in a first-class, sometimes even a luxury, hotel, now in a shabby furnished room.

For three years there had been no record of him anywhere. It was not known in what country or under what name he was operating, assuming that he still was operating.

Maigret walked towards the telephone booth and got Lucas on the phone.

'Go up and see Moers and ask him for all the dope on a man named Moss. Yes. Tell him he's one of our boys. He'll give you his description and all the rest of it. Put out a general alert. But he's not to be arrested. If he's found, they must try not to arouse his suspicion. Get it?'

'I get it, Chief. Someone's just spotted the child again.'

'Where?'

'Avenue Denfert-Rochereau. I've sent someone over. I'm waiting. I haven't got enough men available any more. There's also been a call from the Gare du Nord. Torrence has gone there.'

He felt like walking a bit, in the rain, and went through the Place d'Anvers, where he looked at the bench, now dripping with rain, where Madame Maigret had waited. Opposite, on the building at the corner of the Avenue Trudaine, there was a sign on which was written in big, faded letters the word: *Dentist*.

He would come back. There were so many things he wanted to do which the bustle of events always forced him to postpone to the next day.

He jumped on a bus. When he arrived at his own door, he was astonished not to hear any sound from the kitchen, not to smell anything. He entered, went through the dining-room, where the table wasn't set, and finally saw Madame Maigret, in her petticoat, engaged in taking off her stockings.

This was so unlike her that he didn't know what to say, and she burst out laughing when she saw his big round eyes.

'Are you cross, Maigret?'

Her voice held a tone of almost aggressive good humour which was quite new to him, and on her bed he could see her best dress, her smart hat.

'You'll have to be content with a cold dinner. Just imagine, I've been so busy that I haven't had time to prepare anything. Besides, you so seldom come home to meals, nowadays!'

And, sitting in her easy chair, she was rubbing her feet with a sigh of relief.

'I think I never walked so far in my life!'

He stood there, in his overcoat, his wet hat on his head, looking at her and waiting, and she was deliberately keeping him on tenterhooks.

'I began with the big shops although I was almost sure that was no use. But you never know; and I didn't want to regret my carelessness later. Then I did the whole of the Rue La Fayette, I went up the Rue Notre-Dame-de-Lorette and I walked along the Rue Blanche, the Rue de Clichy. I came back down towards the Opéra, all this on foot, even after it had begun to rain. I suppose I may as well admit that yesterday, without telling you, I'd already "done" the Ternes area and the Champs-Élysées.

'That was to make absolutely sure, too, because I suspected that it was too expensive around there.'

At last he brought out the sentence she was waiting for, which she had been trying to elicit for quite a while.

'What were you looking for?'

'The hat, of course! Didn't you catch on? It was on my mind, that business. I thought it wasn't a man's job. A coat and skirt is a coat and skirt, especially a blue one. But a hat, that's different, and I'd had a good look at this one. They've been wearing white hats for several weeks now. Only one hat is never exactly like another. Do you see? You don't mind if the meal's cold? I brought some cooked meat from the Italian place, Parma ham, pickled mushrooms and a whole lot of ready made hors-d'œuvre.'

'What about the hat?'

'Are you interested in it, Maigret? By the way, your own is dripping on the carpet. You'd better take it off.'

She had been successful, otherwise she wouldn't be in such a teasing mood and would never take the liberty of playing with him like this. He would just have to let her take her

time and maintain his grumpy expression, because she was en-
joying it.

While she was putting on a woollen dress, he sat down on
the edge of the bed.

'I knew it wasn't a hat from a really first-class milliner and
that there was no sense in looking in the Rue de la Paix, the
Rue Saint-Honoré or the Avenue Matignon. Anyhow, those
places don't put anything in the window, and I'd have had to
go in and pretend to be a customer. Can you see me trying on
hats at Caroline Reboux' or Rose Valois'?

'But it wasn't a hat from the Galeries or the Printemps either.

'Somewhere between the two. A hat from a milliner's definitely, and a milliner with good taste.

'That's why I did all the little shops, especially around the
Place d'Anvers, or not too far away at all events.

'I saw at least a hundred white hats, and yet it was a pearl
grey one that finally stopped me, in the Rue Caumartin, at
"Hélène et Rosine".

'It was exactly the same hat in another shade, and I'm sure
I'm not mistaken. I told you that the one belonging to the lady
with the little boy had a tiny veil, three or four fingers wide,
that came down just over the eyes.

'The grey hat had the same veil.'

'Did you go in?'

Maigret had to make an effort not to smile, for it was the
first time that the shy Madame Maigret had taken part in an
investigation, no doubt also the first time she had entered a
milliner's in the neighbourhood of the Opéra.

'Are you surprised? Do you think I look too much of a
stay-at-home? Yes, I did go in. I was afraid it might be closed.
I asked perfectly naturally if they hadn't got the same hat in
white.

'The lady said not, but they had it in pale blue, yellow and jade green. She added that she had had it in white, but that she had sold it more than a month ago.'

'What did you do?' he asked, intrigued.

'I heaved a deep sigh and said to her:

'"That must have been the one I saw a friend of mine wearing."

'I could see myself in the glass, because there are mirrors all round the shop, and my face was scarlet.

'"Do you know Countess Panetti?" she asked, in a tone of surprise that wasn't very flattering.

'"I've met her. I'd very much like to see her again, because I have some information for her which she asked me to get and I've mislaid her address."

'"I suppose she's still at . . ."

'She was on the point of stopping. She wasn't completely sure of me. But she couldn't very well not finish her sentence.

'"I suppose she's still at Claridge's."'

Madame Maigret was looking at him triumphantly and teasingly at the same time, with an anxious trembling of her lips in spite of everything. He kept up the game to the end, muttered:

'I hope you didn't go interrogating the hall porter at Claridge's.'

'I came straight back. Are you cross?'

'No.'

'I've caused you enough trouble with this business so the least I can do is try to help you. Now come and eat, since I hope you're going to take time for a bite before you go over there.'

This dinner reminded him of their first meals together, when she was discovering Paris and was delighted by all the little ready-to-eat dishes sold in the Italian shops. It was more like a picnic than a dinner.

'Do you think the information's reliable?'

'So long as you didn't get the wrong hat.'

'I'm absolutely sure about that. As far as the shoes go, I'm not so confident.'

'What's this about shoes now?'

'When you're sitting on a bench, in a square, your eyes naturally fall on the shoes of the person next to you. Once when I looked at them closely I could see that she was embarrassed and was trying to stick her feet under the bench.'

'Why?'

'I'll explain, Maigret. Don't make that face! It's not your fault if you don't know anything about feminine matters. Suppose someone accustomed to first-class couturiers wants to look like a little housewife and be inconspicuous? She buys a ready made suit, which is easy. She may also buy a hat that isn't in the luxury class, although I'm not quite so sure about the hat.'

'What do you mean?'

'She may already have had it, but thought it looked enough like the other white hats being worn this season by shopgirls. She takes off her jewellery, of course! But there's one thing she would have a lot of trouble getting used to: ready made shoes. Having your shoes made to measure by the best shoemakers makes your feet delicate. You've heard me groaning often enough to know that women have sensitive feet by nature. So the lady keeps her own shoes, thinking no one will notice them. That's where she's wrong, because, as far as I'm concerned, that's the first thing I look at. Usually it happens the other way round: you see pretty, well-dressed women, with expensive frocks or fur coats, wearing cheap shoes.'

'Did she have expensive shoes?'

'Made to measure, I'm sure. I don't know enough about it to say what shoemaker they came from. No doubt some women could have told.'

He took time after dinner to pour himself a little glass of *prunelle* and to smoke almost a whole pipe.

'Are you going to Claridge's? You won't be too late?'

He took a cab, got out opposite the luxury hotel on the Champs-Élysées and walked over to the hall porter's office. It was the night porter by this time, whom he had known for years, and this was a good thing because night porters invariably know more about the guests than those on the day shift.

His arrival in a place of this type always produced the same effect. He could see the clerks at the reception desk, the assistant manager and even the lift boy raising their eyebrows and wondering what was up. Scandals are unpopular in a luxury hotel, and the presence of a chief-inspector from Police Headquarters rarely bodes any good.

'How are you, Benoît?'

'Not too bad, Monsieur Maigret. The Americans are beginning to show up.'

'Is Countess Panetti still here?'

'It's at least a month since she left. Would you like me to check the exact date?'

'Did her family go with her?'

'What family?'

It was the slack time. Most of the guests were out, at the theatre or at dinner. In the golden light the pages stood about, with their arms dangling, near the marble columns and observed the chief-inspector, whom they all knew by sight, from a distance.

'I never knew she had any family. She's been stopping here for years now . . . and . . .'

'Tell me, have you ever seen the Countess in a white hat?'

'Certainly. She received one a few days before her departure.'

'Did she also wear a blue suit?'

'No. You must have got them mixed up, Monsieur Maigret. The blue suit is her maid, or her companion if you prefer it, in any case the young lady who travels with her.'

'You've never seen Countess Panetti in a blue suit?'

'If you knew her you wouldn't ask me that.'

Just on the off-chance, Maigret handed him the photographs of the women picked out by Moers.

'Anyone there who looks like her?'

Benoît looked at the chief-inspector, flabbergasted.

'Are you sure you're not mistaken? You're showing me photographs of women under thirty, and the countess isn't much less than seventy. Look, you'd better find out what your colleagues in the Society Section have got on her, because they must know her.'

'We get all kinds, don't we? Well, the countess is one of our most unusual guests.'

'In the first place, do you know who she is?'

'She's the widow of Count Panetti, the munitions and heavy industry man in Italy.'

'She lives all over the place, Paris, Cannes, Egypt. I think she spends some time every year in Vichy, too.'

'Does she drink?'

'Shall we say she uses champagne instead of water? I wouldn't be surprised if she brushed her teeth with Pommery Brut! She dresses like a young girl, makes up like a doll and spends most of every night in nightclubs.'

'Her maid?'

'I don't know much about her. She's always getting new ones. I hadn't seen this one until this year. Last year she had a big girl with red hair, a professional masseuse, because she used to take a massage every day.'

'Do you know the girl's name?'

'Gloria something. I haven't got her slip any more, but they'll tell you in the office. I don't know if she's Italian or just from the South, maybe even from Toulouse?'

'Small and dark?'

'Yes, a smart, decent, pretty girl. I didn't see much of her. She lived in the suite, not in a servant's room, and she had her meals with her employer.'

'No man?'

'Only the son-in-law, who came to see them from time to time.'

'When?'

'Not long before they left. Ask at the desk for the dates. He didn't live in the hotel.'

'Do you know his name?'

'Krynker, I think. He's a Czech or a Hungarian.'

'Dark, rather heavy, around forty?'

'No. On the contrary, very fair and much younger. I doubt that he's more than thirty.'

They were interrupted by a group of American women in evening dress depositing their keys and asking for a taxi.

'As for swearing that he was really a son-in-law . . .'

'Did she have affairs?'

'I don't know. I can't say yes or no.'

'Did the son-in-law ever spend the night here?'

'No. But they went out together several times.'

'With the companion?'

'She never went out at night with the countess. I've never even seen her in evening dress.'

'Do you know where they went?'

'To London, if I remember right. But just a minute. Something's coming back to me. Ernest! Come here. There's nothing to be afraid of. Didn't Countess Panetti leave her heavy luggage behind?'

'Yes, sir.'

The porter explained:

'It often happens that our guests who are going away for a fairly long time leave some of their luggage here. We have a special baggage room for it. The countess left her trunks there.'

'She didn't say when she would be back?'

'Not that I know of.'

'Did she leave alone?'

'With her maid.'

'In a taxi?'

'You'd have to ask my opposite number on the day shift about that. You'll find him here tomorrow morning from eight o'clock on.'

Maigret took out of his pocket the photograph of Moss. The hall porter merely glanced at it, pulled a face.

'You won't find him here.'

'Do you know him?'

'Paterson. I did know him, under the name of Mosselaer, when I was working in Milan at least fifteen years ago. He's barred from all the luxury hotels and he wouldn't dare show his face in them. He knows they wouldn't give him a room, wouldn't even allow him to walk through the hall.'

'You haven't seen him recently?'

'No. If I did run into him, I'd start by asking him for the hundred lire he borrowed from me years ago and never returned.'

'Is the day porter on the telephone?'

'You can always try to ring him at his villa at Saint-Cloud, but he hardly ever answers. He doesn't like to be disturbed in the evening and he usually takes the phone off the hook.'

Nevertheless he did answer, and the music from the radio was audible over the telephone too.

'The head baggage-porter could give you more accurate information, I'm sure. I don't remember having a cab called for her.

Generally, when she leaves the hotel, she gets me to look after her Pullman or air tickets.'

'You didn't do so this time?'

'No. It's only just struck me. Maybe she left in a private car.'

'You don't know whether the son-in-law, Krynker, owned a car?'

'Certainly he did! A big chocolate-coloured American one.'

'Thank you. I'll probably see you tomorrow morning.'

He went over to the desk, where the assistant manager in his black coat and striped trousers insisted on finding the registration slips himself.

'She left the hotel on February 16, during the evening. I have her bill right here.'

'Was she alone?'

'I see two luncheons down for that day. So she must have eaten with her companion.'

'Would you please lend me this bill?'

It showed the daily expenditures of the countess at the hotel, and Maigret wanted to study them at leisure.

'On condition you give it back to me! Otherwise we'll be in trouble with the income tax boys. By the way, how do the police come to be interested in a personality like Countess Panetti?'

Maigret, his mind on something else, almost replied: 'All because of my wife!'

He caught himself in time, and muttered:

'I don't know yet. Something about a hat.'

Chapter Six

Maigret was pushing the revolving door, catching sight of the garlands of lights on the Champs-Élysées which, in the rain, always made him think of moist eyes; he was about to start walking down to the Rond-Point when he raised his eyebrows. Leaning against a tree trunk, not far from a flower girl who was sheltering from the rain, Janvier was watching him, pathetic, comical, looking as if he were trying to get something across to him.

He walked up to him.

'What in the world are you doing here?'

The inspector indicated a silhouette outlined against one of the few illuminated shop-windows. It was Alfonsi, who seemed intensely interested in a display of luggage.

'He's following you. So that I have to be following you too.'

'Did he see Liotard, after his visit to the Rue de Turenne?'

'No. He phoned him.'

'Call it a day. Do you want me to drop you at home?'

Janvier lived not far out of his way, in the Rue Réaumur.

Alfonsi watched them walk off together, seemed surprised, taken aback, then, as Maigret was hailing a cab, decided to turn back and went off in the direction of the Étoile.

'Anything new?'

'Any amount. Too much, almost.'

'Do you want me to take care of Alfonsi again tomorrow morning?'

'No. Drop in at the office. There'll probably be plenty of work for everybody.'

When the inspector had got out, Maigret said to the driver:

'Drive through the Rue de Turenne.'

It wasn't late. He vaguely hoped he would see a light at the bookbinder's. This would have been the ideal time for the long chat with Fernande that he had been hankering after for quite a while.

Because of a gleam of light on the glass door he got out of the cab, but realized that the interior was in darkness, hesitated to knock, set off again in the direction of the Quai des Orfèvres, where Torrence was on duty, and gave him some instructions.

Madame Maigret had just gone to bed when he tiptoed in. As he was undressing in the dark so as not to wake her, she asked:

'The hat?'

'It was bought by Countess Panetti all right.'

'Did you see her?'

'No. But she's about seventy-five.'

He went to bed in a bad temper, or preoccupied, and it was still raining when he awoke; then he cut himself shaving.

'Are you going on with your investigation?' he asked his wife who, in curlers, was serving his breakfast.

'Is there anything else for me to do?' she inquired seriously.

'I don't know. Now that you've started . . .'

He bought his paper at the corner of the Boulevard Voltaire, found no new statement by Philippe Liotard in it, no new challenge. The night porter at Claridge's had been discreet, for there was no mention of the countess either.

Back at the Quai, Lucas, relieving Torrence, had received his instructions, and the machine was functioning; they were now looking for the Italian countess on the Riviera and in foreign capitals, while inquiries were also being made about the man named Krynker and the maid.

On the bus platform, enveloped in fine rain, a passenger facing him was reading his paper, and this paper carried a headline which gave the chief-inspector something to think about.

INQUIRY DRAGS

How many people, at that very minute, were actively engaged on it? Railway stations, ports, airports were still under observation. Hotels and boarding-houses were continuously being searched. Not only in Paris and in France, but in London, Brussels, Amsterdam, Rome, they were trying to pick up the track of Alfred Moss.

Maigret got out at the Rue de Turenne, entered the 'Tabac des Vosges' to buy a packet of tobacco and took the opportunity of drinking a glass of white wine. There were no reporters, nothing but local residents who were beginning to pipe down a bit.

The bookbinder's door was locked. He knocked, and soon saw Fernande emerging from the basement by the spiral staircase. In curlers, like Madame Maigret, she hesitated when she recognized him through the glass and finally came and opened the door.

'I'd like to talk to you for a few minutes.'

It was chilly on the stairs, since the furnace had not been relighted.

'Wouldn't you rather come downstairs?'

He followed her into the kitchen, which she had been in the middle of cleaning when he had disturbed her.

She, too, seemed tired, with something like discouragement in her expression.

'Would you like a cup of coffee? I have some hot.'

He accepted, sat down by the table, and she finally sat down facing him, wrapping the folds of her dressing-gown around her bare legs.

'Alfonsi came to see you yesterday. What does he want?'

'I don't know. He's interested mainly in the questions you asked me, keeps telling me not to trust you.'

'Did you mention the poisoning attempt to him?'

'Yes.'

'Why?'

'You didn't tell me not to. I can't remember how it came up in the conversation. He's working for Liotard and it seems all right for him to be kept informed.'

'No one else has been to see you?'

It seemed to him that the Fleming's wife hesitated, but it may have been the effect of weariness weighing upon her. She had helped herself to a big bowl of coffee. She probably relied on black coffee in copious amounts to keep her going.

'No. Nobody.'

'Did you tell your husband why you're not bringing his meals any more?'

'I managed to let him know. Thanks to you.'

'No one's rung you up?'

'No. I don't think so. I hear the bell occasionally. But by the time I get upstairs there's no one on the line.'

Then he took from his pocket the photograph of Alfred Moss.

'Do you recognize this man?'

She looked at the photograph, then at Maigret, and said quite naturally:

'Of course.'

'Who is it?'

'It's Alfred, my husband's brother.'

'Is it long since you last saw him?'

'I hardly ever see him. Sometimes he doesn't come here for more than a year. He lives abroad most of the time.'

'Do you know what he does?'

'Not exactly. Frans says he's an unfortunate character, a failure, who never had any luck.'

'He never mentioned his profession?'

'I know he worked in a circus, that he was an acrobat and broke his spine in a fall.'

'And since then?'

'Isn't he some kind of impresario?'

'Did you know he didn't call himself Steuvels like his brother, but Moss? Have you ever been told why?'

'Yes.'

She was reluctant to go on, looked at the picture which Maigret had left on the kitchen table, near the coffee bowls, then she got up to turn off the gas under a saucepan of water.

'I couldn't help guessing part of it. Perhaps if you questioned Frans on this subject he'd tell you more. You know that his parents were very poor, but that's not the whole story. Actually his mother was in the same game I used to be in myself, at Ghent, or rather in a shady district just outside the town.

'She drank, into the bargain. I wonder if she wasn't half-crazy. She had seven or eight children and half the time she didn't know who their father was.

'It was Frans who chose the name Steuvels later. His mother's name was Mosselaer.'

'Is she dead?'

'I think so. He avoids mentioning her.'

'Has he kept in touch with his brothers and sisters?'

'I don't think so. Alfred's the only one who comes to see him from time to time, pretty seldom. He must have his ups and downs because sometimes he seems prosperous, he's well dressed, gets out of a taxi in front of the house and brings presents, while other times he's quite shabby.'

'When did you last see him?'

'Let me think. It must be two months ago at least.'

'Did he stay to dinner?'

'Yes, as a matter of course.'

'Tell me, on the occasion of these visits, did your husband ever try to get rid of you under any pretext?'

'No. Why? They were sometimes in the workshop by themselves, but from downstairs, where I was cooking, I could hear what they said.'

'What did they talk about?'

'Nothing particular. Moss liked to reminisce about the time when he was an acrobat and the different countries he'd lived in. And he was also the one who nearly always made allusions to their childhood and their mother, and that's how I picked up the few things I know.'

'Alfred is the younger, I suppose?'

'Three or four years younger. Afterwards Frans would sometimes walk to the corner of the street with him. That's the only time I wasn't with them.'

'They never talked business?'

'Never.'

'Alfred never came with friends either, male or female?'

'He was always alone. I think he'd been married once. I'm not sure. It seems to me he mentioned it. In any case, he'd been in love with a woman, and she'd made him unhappy.'

It was warm and quiet in the little kitchen from which you couldn't see the outside world at all and where the light had to be kept on all day. Maigret would have liked to have Frans Steuvels there facing him and to talk to him as he was talking to his wife.

'You told me last time I was here that he practically never

went out without you. Yet he went to the bank from time to time.'

'I don't call that going out. It's just around the corner. He only had to walk across the Place des Vosges.'

'Otherwise you were together from morning to night?'

'Just about. I'd go shopping, of course, but always close by. Once in a blue moon I'd go into town to buy a few things. I'm not very stylish, as you may have noticed.'

'You never went to see relatives?'

'I only have my mother and my sister at Concarneau, and it took a fake telegram to get me to go and visit them.'

It was as though something were bothering Maigret.

'There's no day when you're regularly out?'

She, in turn, seemed to be striving to follow his train of thought and to answer accordingly.

'No. Except for laundry day, of course.'

'You don't do the laundry here?'

'Where could I do it? I have to go up to the ground floor for water. I can't hang up the washing in the workshop, and it wouldn't dry in a basement. Once a week in summer, and once a fortnight in winter, I go to the laundry-boat on the Seine.'

'Whereabouts?'

'Square du Vert-Galant. You know, just below the Pont-Neuf. It takes me half a day. The next morning I go to fetch the washing, which is dry and ready to iron.'

Visibly, Maigret was relaxing, smoking his pipe with more pleasure, and his expression had become livelier.

'In fact, one day a week in summer, one day every two weeks in winter, Frans was alone here.'

'Not all day.'

'Did you go to the laundry-boat in the morning or the afternoon?'

'Afternoon. I tried going in the morning, but it was difficult, on account of the cleaning and cooking.'

'Have you got a key to the house?'

'Of course.'

'Did you often have to use it?'

'What do you mean?'

'Did it sometimes happen that when you came back your husband wasn't in the workshop?'

'Hardly ever.'

'But it did happen?'

'I think so. Yes.'

'Recently?'

She had just thought of it, too, for she hesitated.

'The week I went to Concarneau.'

'When's your laundry day?'

'Monday.'

'Did he come home long after you?'

'Not long. Maybe an hour.'

'Did you ask him where he'd been?'

'I never ask him anything. He's free. It's not my place to ask him questions.'

'You don't know whether he left the neighbourhood? Weren't you worried?'

'I was at the door when he came back. I saw him get out of the bus on the corner of the Rue des Francs-Bourgeois.'

'The bus coming from the centre or from the Bastille?'

'From the centre.'

'So far as I can tell from this photo, the two brothers are the same height?'

'Yes. Alfred looks slimmer because he has a thin face, but his body is more muscular. They're not alike in features, except that they both have red hair. But from behind, the resemblance is striking, and I've occasionally mistaken one for the other.'

97

'The times when you saw Alfred, how was he dressed?'

'That depended, I've told you so already.'

'Do you think he may have borrowed money from his brother?'

'I've thought of that, but it doesn't seem likely. Not in front of me, in any case.'

'On his last visit, wasn't he wearing a blue suit?'

She looked him in the eye. She had caught on.

'I'm almost sure he was wearing something dark, but grey rather than blue. When you live by artificial light, you don't pay much attention to colours.'

'How did you manage about money, you and your husband?'

'What money?'

'Did he give you housekeeping money every month?'

'No. When I ran out, I'd ask him for some.'

'He never protested?'

She turned slightly pink.

'He was absent-minded. He always thought he'd given me money just the day before. And then he'd say in astonishment:

' "What, again?" '

'What about your personal things, dresses and hats?'

'I don't spend much, as you know!'

It was her turn to put some questions to him, as if she had been waiting a long time for this moment.

'Listen, chief-inspector, I'm not very intelligent, but I'm not so stupid either. You've questioned me, your detectives have questioned me, and the journalists too, not to mention the tradesmen and the neighbours. A young gentleman of seventeen, who plays amateur detectives, even stopped me in the street and asked me some questions he had written down in a little notebook.

'Once and for all, tell me honestly: do you think Frans is guilty?'

'Guilty of what?'

'You know perfectly well: of having killed a man and burned the body in the furnace?'

He hesitated. He could have given her any answer that came into his head, but he was determined to be honest.

'I have no idea.'

'In that case why is he being kept in prison?'

'In the first place, that's not my responsibility, but the examining magistrate's. And then you mustn't forget that all the circumstantial evidence is against him.'

'The teeth!' she flashed, with irony.

'And above all the bloodstains on the blue suit. Don't forget the suitcase that vanished either.'

'And that I never saw!'

'That doesn't make any difference. Other people saw it, at least a detective did. And then there's the fact that you were called out of town, as if by chance, at that very moment, by a fake telegram. Now, between ourselves, I admit that if it were up to me I'd prefer to let your husband go, but I'd hesitate to release him for the sake of his own safety. You saw what happened yesterday.'

'Yes. That's just what I'm thinking about.'

'Whether he's guilty or innocent, he seems to be in somebody's way.'

'Why did you bring me the photo of his brother?'

'Because, in spite of what you think, that man is quite a dangerous criminal.'

'Has he committed murder?'

'Probably not. That type of man hardly ever kills. But he's wanted by the police of three or four countries, and for more than fifteen years he's been living by stealing and swindling. Are you surprised?'

'No.'

'Did you suspect it?'

'When Frans told me his brother was unfortunate, it seemed to me that he wasn't using the word "unfortunate" in its usual sense. Do you think that Alfred would have been capable of kidnapping a child?'

'I tell you again I have no idea. By the way, have you ever heard of Countess Panetti?'

'Who's she?'

'A very rich Italian woman who lived at Claridge's.'

'Has she been killed too?'

'It's possible, and it's also possible that she's simply away spending the carnival season at Cannes or Nice. I'll know tonight. I'd like to take another look at your husband's account books.'

'Come this way. I've got loads of questions to ask you, but they've slipped my mind. It's when you're not here that I think of them. I ought to write them down like the young man playing detectives.'

She let him precede her upstairs, fetched from a shelf a big black book which the police had examined five or six times.

At the very end an index contained the names of the book-binder's clients, old and new, in alphabetical order. The name Panetti was not listed. Neither was Krynker.

Steuvels had tiny, jerky handwriting, with some letters over-lapping others, a peculiar way of making the *r*'s and *t*'s.

'You've never heard the name Krynker?'

'Not that I remember. Look, we would be together the whole day, but I never assumed the right to ask him questions. Some-times you seem to forget, Chief Inspector, that I'm not just an ordinary wife. Remember where he found me. His action has always amazed me. And now it suddenly occurs to me, as a result of our conversation, that the reason he did it may have been that he remembered what his mother had been.'

Maigret, as if he were no longer listening, was striding towards the door, flinging it open and seizing Alfonsi by the collar of his camel-hair coat.

'Come here, you. You're at it again. Have you decided to spend your days dogging my heels?'

The other man tried to brazen it out, but the chief-inspector had a strong grip on the scruff of his neck, was shaking him like a puppet.

'What are you doing here, just tell me that?'

'I was waiting for you to leave.'

'To come pestering this woman?'

'I have a right to. Provided she chooses to receive me . . .'

'What are you after?'

'Ask Maître Liotard.'

'Liotard or no Liotard, let me tell you one thing: if I catch you following me again, I'll have you pinched for living off a prostitute, mark my words!'

This wasn't an empty threat. Maigret knew very well that the woman Alfonsi lived with spent most of her evenings in Montmartre nightclubs and that she was not unwilling to accompany visiting foreigners to their hotels.

When he came back to Fernande, he looked relieved, and the figure of the ex-detective could be seen making off in the rain towards the Place des Vosges.

'What sort of questions does he ask you?'

'Always the same. He wants to know what you ask me, what I've answered, what you're interested in, what objects you've examined.'

'I think he'll let you alone in future.'

'Do you think Maître Liotard is harming my husband?'

'Whether he is or not, we can't do anything about it at this point.'

He had to go back downstairs, because he had left the

photograph of Moss on the kitchen table. Instead of making for the Quai des Orfèvres, he crossed the street and entered the cobbler's shop.

The latter, at nine in the morning, already had several drinks under his belt and reeked of white wine.

'Well, chief-inspector, everything fine and dandy?'

The two shops were exactly opposite one another. The cobbler and the bookbinder could not help seeing each other every time they raised their eyes, both hunched over their work, with only the width of the street between them.

'Can you remember some of the bookbinder's clients?'

'A few, yes.'

'This one?'

He held the photograph under his nose, while Fernande, opposite, watched them anxiously.

'I call him the clown.'

'Why?'

'I don't know. Because I think he looks like a clown.'

Suddenly he scratched his head, seemed to make a welcome discovery.

'Look here, buy me a drink, and I'll make it worth your while. It was a bit of good luck that you showed me that picture. I mentioned a clown and all of a sudden the word made me think of a suitcase. Why? But of course! Because clowns usually come into the ring with a suitcase.'

'You mean the stooges, don't you?'

'Stooge or clown, it's the same thing. How about the drink?'

'Later.'

'You don't trust me? You're wrong. Honest as a new-born babe, that's what I always say. Well, anyhow, there's no doubt that the fellow with the suitcase is your man.'

'What fellow with the suitcase?'

The cobbler gave him a wink which was meant to be knowing.

'You're not going to try any tricks with me, are you? I suppose I don't read the papers, do I? Well, what were the papers concerned with, right at the start? Didn't people come asking me whether I'd seen Frans go out with a suitcase, or his wife, or anyone else?'

'And you did see the man in the photo go out with the suitcase?'

'Not that day, anyhow, not that I noticed. But I'm thinking of the other times.'

'Did he come here often?'

'Yes, often.'

'Once a week, for example? Or once a fortnight?'

'Maybe. I don't want to make anything up, because I know what a rough time the lawyers'll give me if this ever comes up in court. He used to come here often that's all I'm saying.'

'In the morning? Afternoon?'

'My answer to that is: the afternoon. Do you know why? Because I can remember seeing him when the lights were on, so it must have been afternoon. He always had a small suitcase with him.'

'Brown?'

'Probably. Aren't most suitcases brown? He would sit down in a corner of the workshop, waiting for the job to be finished, and he'd leave again with the suitcase.'

'Did that take long?'

'I don't know. More than an hour in any case. Sometimes it seemed to me that he stayed the whole afternoon.'

'Did he always come on the same day?'

'I can't tell you that either.'

'Think before you answer. Did you ever see this man in the studio at the same time as Madame Steuvels?'

'At the same time as Fernande? Wait. I can't call it to mind. Once, at least, the two men went out together, and Frans closed his shop.'

'Recently?'

'I'll have to think. When are we going to have that drink?'

Maigret had no alternative but to follow him to the 'Grand Turenne', where the cobbler assumed a triumphant manner.

'Two old marcs. On the chief-inspector!'

He drank three, one after another, and was trying to start telling about the clown all over again by the time Maigret managed to get rid of him. When he passed the bookbinder's workshop, Fernande was watching him, through the glass door, with an air of reproach.

But he had to keep on with his job to the end. He entered the concierge's lodge, where she was busy peeling potatoes.

'Well! So you're around again!' she observed tartly, offended at having been neglected for so long.

'Do you know this man?'

She went to fetch her glasses from the drawer.

'I don't know his name, if that's what you mean, but I've seen him before. Didn't the cobbler give you the information?'

She was jealous because other people had been questioned first.

'Have you seen him often?'

'I've seen him, that's all I know.'

'Was he a client of the bookbinder?'

'I suppose so, seeing he came to his shop.'

'He didn't come on any other occasion?'

'I think he occasionally came to dinner with them, but I pay so little attention to my tenants!'

The stationer across the street, the cardboard manufacturer, the umbrella seller, in short, the routine, always the same

question, the same gesture, the picture, which people examined gravely. Some hesitated. Others had seen the man without
remembering where or in what circumstances.

Just as he was leaving the neighbourhood, Maigret had an
impulse to push open the door of the 'Tabac des Vosges' one
last time.

'Have you ever seen that mug before, *patron*?'

The barkeeper did not hesitate.

'The man with the suitcase!' he said.

'Explain.'

'I don't know what he sells, but he must be a door-to-door
salesman. He used to come in quite often, always a little while
after lunch. He'd drink strawberry syrup with Vichy water and
he explained to me that he had a stomach ulcer.'

'Would he stay long?'

'Sometimes a quarter of an hour, sometimes longer. Look,
he always sat there, near the door.'

From where you could keep an eye on the corner of the Rue
de Turenne!

'He must have been waiting till it was time for an appointment with a customer. Once, not so long ago, he stayed almost
an hour and finally asked for a telephone *jeton*.'

'You don't know whom he rang up?'

'No. When he came back it was only to leave again straight
away.'

'In which direction?'

'I wasn't paying attention.'

As a reporter was coming in, the *patron* asked Maigret in an
undertone:

'Is it all right to talk about it?'

Maigret shrugged. There was no point in making mysteries,
now that the cobbler was in the know.

'If you want to.'

When he entered Lucas's office, the latter was coping with two telephones, and Maigret had to wait quite a while.

'I'm still hunting for the countess,' sighed the sergeant, mopping his forehead. 'The Wagons-Lits Company, who know her quite well, haven't seen her on any of their lines for several months. I've had most of the big hotels at Cannes, Nice, Antibes and Villefranche on the line. Nothing doing. I've also rung the casinos, where she hasn't set foot. Lapointe, who speaks English, is telephoning Scotland Yard at this moment, and someone or other is taking care of the Italians.'

Before going in to see Judge Dossin, Maigret went upstairs to have a word with Moers and return the useless photographs.

'No results?' asked poor Moers.

'One out of three, that's not bad; now we only have to round up the other two, but it's possible that they've never been through an identification check.'

At noon, they were still not on the track of Countess Panetti, and two Italian journalists who had been tipped off were waiting, greatly excited, outside the door to Maigret's office.

Chapter Seven

Madame Maigret had been rather surprised when on Saturday, about three o'clock, her husband had telephoned to find out whether dinner was cooking.

'Not yet. Why? . . . Yes, of course I'd like to. If you're sure you'll be free. Quite sure? All right. I'll get dressed. I'll be there. Near the clock, yes. No, no sauerkraut for me, but I'd love a *potée lorraine*. What? You're not joking, are you? Are you serious, Maigret? Anywhere I like? That's too good to be true, and I feel sure you're going to ring again in an hour to tell me you won't be home to dinner or till morning. Oh well! I'll get ready anyway.'

So that instead of smelling of cooking, that Saturday, the flat on the Boulevard Richard-Lenoir had smelled of bath water, eau-de-cologne and the sweetish scent which Madame Maigret kept for special occasions.

Maigret was at the meeting place almost on time, within five minutes, at the Alsatian restaurant in the Rue d'Enghien where they had sometimes been to have dinner, and, relaxed, with the air of thinking about the same things as other men, he had eaten sauerkraut prepared just the way he liked it.

'Have you decided on the cinema?'

Because, and this was what had made Madame Maigret so incredulous just now on the telephone, he had invited her to spend the evening at any cinema she chose.

They went to the Paramount on the Boulevard des Italiens, and the chief-inspector queued up for the tickets without grumbling, emptied his pipe in an enormous spittoon as they went in.

They heard the electric organ, saw the orchestra emerge from the floor on a platform while a curtain transformed itself into a sort of synthetic sunset. It was not until after the cartoons that Madame Maigret understood. The trailer of the next film had just been shown, then some short reels advertising some kind of sweet snack and furniture on hire-purchase.

The Prefecture of Police informs us . . .

It was the first time she had seen this announcement on the screen, and immediately afterwards an identification photograph was projected, first full face, then in profile, showing Alfred Moss, whose successive aliases were listed.

Anybody having met this man in the course of the last two months is requested to telephone immediately . . .

'So that was it?' she said, out in the street again, while they were going part of the way home on foot in order to get some fresh air.

'That wasn't the only reason. The idea, by the way, isn't mine. It was suggested to the Prefect ages ago, but there had never been an opportunity to try it out until now. Moers had noticed that photographs published in the papers are always more or less distorted because of the half-tone screen and the inking. Film projection, on the other hand, by enlarging the smallest characteristics, makes a more striking impression.'

'Anyway, whether that was the reason or not, it turned out nicely for me. How long is it since we did this?'

'Three weeks?' he suggested in all sincerity.

'Exactly two and a half months!'

They bickered a bit, in fun. And next morning, because of the sun which was again brilliant and springlike, Maigret had sung in his bath. He had walked all the way to the Quai, through the almost deserted streets, and it was always a pleasure to find the wide corridors of Police Headquarters with their doors standing open on vacant offices.

Lucas had only just arrived. Torrence was there too, as was Janvier; it wasn't long before little Lapointe appeared, but because it was Sunday they seemed to be working like amateurs. Perhaps also because it was Sunday, they left the communicating doors open, and from time to time, by way of music, they heard the bells of the local churches.

Lapointe had been the only one to bring in any new information. The previous night, before leaving, Maigret had asked him:

'By the way, where does that young journalist live who's carrying on with your sister?'

'He's stopped going out with her. You mean Antoine Bizard.'

'They've broken up?'

'I don't know. Perhaps I've scared him?'

'I'd like his address.'

'I don't know it. I know where he eats most of his meals and I doubt that my sister knows any more. I'll inquire from the newspaper offices.'

As he entered, he handed a slip of paper to Maigret. This was the address in question, Rue Bergère, in the same block as Philippe Liotard.

'That's fine, son. Thanks,' the chief-inspector had simply said, without adding any comment.

If it had been a bit warmer, he would have taken off his coat just for the sake of being in his shirt-sleeves like people who potter around all day on Sunday, for pottering around was just what he felt like. All his pipes were lined up on his desk, and he had taken out of his pocket his fat black notebook which he always stuffed full of notes but practically never consulted.

Two or three times he had thrown into the waste-paper basket the big sheets on which he had scribbled. Ruled a set of columns to start with. Then changed his mind.

In the end his work had taken a turn for the better.

> *Thursday, February 15 – Countess Panetti, accompanied by her maid, Gloria Lotti, leaves Claridge's in the chocolate-coloured Chrysler of her son-in-law Krynker.*

The date had been confirmed by the daytime hall porter. As for the car, the information had been furnished by one of the hotel carmen who had reported the time of departure as seven o'clock at night. He had added that the old lady seemed worried and that her son-in-law was hurrying her as if they were about to miss a train or an important appointment.

Still no trace of the countess. He went into Lucas's office to make sure; the sergeant was still receiving reports from all over the place.

The Italian journalists, the night before, had obtained only a few scraps of information from the police, had furnished a few themselves; they did in fact know Countess Panetti. The marriage of her only daughter, Bella, had caused a big stir in Italy, because, lacking her mother's consent, the girl had run away from home to get married at Monte Carlo.

That was five years ago, and since then the two women refused to meet.

If Krynker was in Paris, said the Italian journalists, it was probably to attempt another reconciliation.

> *Friday, February 16 – Gloria Lotti, who is wearing the countess's white hat, goes to Concarneau, from where she*

*sends a telegram to Fernande Steuvels and from where she
returns the same night without having met anyone.*

In the margin Maigret had amused himself by drawing a
woman's hat with a tiny veil.

*Saturday, February 17 – at noon Fernande leaves the Rue de
Turenne and departs for Concarneau. Her husband does not
accompany her to the station. About four o'clock a customer
comes to call for some work he has commissioned and finds
Frans Steuvels in his workshop where nothing seems out of
the ordinary. Asked about the suitcase, he doesn't remember
having seen it.*

*At a few minutes past eight, three persons, among them
Alfred Moss and probably the man who is later to register in
the Rue Lepic under the name of Levine, are taken by taxi
from the Gare Saint-Lazare to the corner of the Rue de
Turenne and the Rue des Francs-Bourgeois.*

*The concierge hears knocking at Steuvels's door just before
nine o'clock. She has the impression that the three men
entered.*

In the margin, in red pencil, he wrote: *Is the third character
Krynker?*

*Sunday, February 18 – The furnace, not in use for the last few
days, has been going all night, and Frans Steuvels has to
make at least five trips into the courtyard to carry the ashes
to the dustbins.*

*Mademoiselle Béguin, the tenant on the fourth floor, was
inconvenienced by the smoke, 'which had a funny smell'.*

*Monday, February 19 – The furnace is still going. The
bookbinder is at home alone all day.*

*Tuesday, February 20 – Police Headquarters receives an
anonymous note about a man having been burned in the*

bookbinder's furnace. Fernande returns from Concarneau.

Wednesday, February 21 – Lapointe's visit to the Rue de Turenne. He sees the suitcase with the handle mended with string under a table in the workshop. Lapointe leaves the workshop about noon. Has lunch with his sister and talks to her about the case. Does Mademoiselle Lapointe meet her young man, Antoine Bizard, who lives in the same building as the briefless lawyer Liotard? Or does she telephone him?

In the afternoon, before five, the lawyer calls at the Rue de Turenne under the pretext of ordering an ex libris.

When Lucas makes his search, at five o'clock, the suitcase has disappeared.

Interrogation of Steuvels at Headquarters. Towards the end of the night he names Maître Liotard as his lawyer.

Maigret stood up for a little stroll, a glance at the notes the inspectors were taking at the telephones. It wasn't time yet to have beer sent up, and he simply filled another pipe instead.

Thursday, February 22.
Friday, February 23.
Saturday . . .

A whole column of dates with nothing opposite them, except that the inquiry was dragging, the papers were agitating, Liotard, snapping like a cur, was attacking the police in general and Maigret in particular. The right-hand column remained empty until:

Sunday, March 10 – A man named Levine rents a room at the Hôtel Beauséjour in the Rue Lepic and moves in with a little boy of about two.

Gloria Lotti, who passes for the nursemaid, looks after the child, whom she takes out every morning for an airing in the Place d'Anvers while Levine is asleep.

She does not sleep at the hotel, which she leaves very late when Levine comes home.

Monday, March 11 – Ditto.

Tuesday, March 12 – Half past nine: Gloria and the child leave the Hôtel Beauséjour as usual. Quarter past ten: Moss appears at the hotel and asks for Levine. The latter immediately packs and brings down his luggage while Moss remains alone in the room.

Five minutes to eleven: Gloria sees Levine and instantly leaves the child who remains in the charge of Madame Maigret. A little after eleven she enters the Beauséjour with her companion. They join Moss and all three of them argue for more than an hour. Moss leaves first. At a quarter to one Gloria and Levine leave the hotel and Gloria gets into a taxi alone. She goes back to the Square d'Anvers and picks up the child. She takes the taxi as far as the Porte de Neuilly, then says she wants to go to the Gare Saint-Lazare and suddenly stops in the Place Saint-Augustin, where she gets into another taxi. She leaves this one, still with the little boy, at the corner of the Faubourg Montmartre and the Grands Boulevards.

The page was ornamental, for Maigret was decorating it with drawings like a child's.

On another sheet he noted the dates on which they had lost track of the various characters.

Countess Panetti . . . February 16.

The carman at Claridge's had been the last to see her, when she had stepped into her son-in-law's chocolate-coloured Chrysler.

Krynker!

Maigret hesitated to write down the date Saturday, February 17, for they had no proof at all that he was the third person dropped by the taxi at the corner of the Rue de Turenne.

If that were not he, his tracks disappeared simultaneously with the old lady's.

Alfred Moss ... Tuesday, March 12.

He had been the first to leave the Hôtel Beauséjour, about noon.

Levine ... Tuesday, March 12.

Half an hour after the preceding character, when he saw Gloria into a taxi.

Gloria and the child ... Same date.

Two hours later, in the crowd, at the Carrefour Montmartre.

Today was Sunday, March 17. Since the 12th there had been nothing new to report. Except for the investigation.

Or rather there was one date to note, which he added to the column:

Friday, March 15 – Somebody in the métro tries (!) to pour some poison into the dinner prepared for Frans Steuvels.

But that was still in doubt. The experts had found no trace of poison. In the state of nervous exhaustion Fernande had been in recently, she might well have mistaken a passenger's clumsiness for a suspicious action.

In any case it wasn't Moss popping up again, for she would have recognized him.

Levine?

Suppose it was a message, and not poison, that someone had tried to slip into the casserole?

Maigret, with a sunbeam catching him in the face, made a

few more little drawings, screwing up his eyes, then he went
to look at a string of barges going past on the Seine, at the Pont
Saint-Michel, with families dressed in their Sunday clothes
crossing it.

Madame Maigret had probably gone back to bed, as she
sometimes did on Sundays, simply to make it seem more like
Sunday, for she was incapable of going back to sleep.

'Janvier! What about ordering some beer?'

Janvier rang the 'Brasserie Dauphine', where the *patron*
asked as a matter of course:

'And some sandwiches?'

By means of a discreet telephone call, Maigret discovered
that Judge Dossin, punctilious, was in his office; he too, no
doubt, like the chief-inspector, hoping to sort things out in
peace.

'Still no news of the car?'

It was amusing to think that on this beautiful Sunday, which
smelled of spring, in all the villages where people were emerging from Mass or from little cafés, hard-working policemen
were keeping an eye on the cars and looking for the chocolate-
coloured Chrysler.

'May I look, chief?' asked Lucas, who had come to stretch
his legs in Maigret's office between telephone calls.

He examined the chief-inspector's work carefully, shook his
head.

'Why didn't you ask me? I've drawn up the same diagram, in
more detail.'

'But without the little drawings!' Maigret joked. 'What's the
leading item in the phone calls? Cars? Moss?'

'Cars for the moment. Lots of chocolate-coloured cars. Unfortunately, when I pin them down, they're no longer exactly
chocolate-coloured, they turn reddish-brown, or else they're
Citroëns, Peugeots. We check anyhow. The suburbs are

beginning to phone in now, and the radius is expanding to about sixty miles from Paris.'

In a little while, thanks to the radio, all France would be in on it. There was nothing to do but wait, and that wasn't so disagreeable. The waiter from the café brought a huge tray covered with glasses of beer, piles of sandwiches, and there was every chance that he would make similar trips up before the day was out.

They were in the midst of eating and drinking and they had just opened the windows, for the sun was warm, when they saw Moers come in, blinking his eyes, as though he were emerging from a dark place.

They hadn't known he was in the building, where, theoretically, he had no business. Yet here he was coming from upstairs, where he must be the only person in the laboratories.

'I'm sorry to bother you.'

'A glass of beer? There's one left.'

'No thanks. As I was falling asleep, an idea kept bothering me. We were so sure that the blue suit unquestionably belonged to Steuvels that we examined it only for bloodstains. As the suit's still up there, I came in this morning to do an analysis of the dust.'

This was, in fact, a routine procedure which no one had thought of in the present case. Moers had sealed each piece of clothing in a strong paper bag to which he had given a good beating, so as to extract every trace of dust from the cloth.

'You've found something?'

'Sawdust, very fine, in remarkable quantities. It's really more like wood powder.'

'The kind you might get in a sawmill?'

'No. That kind of sawdust would be less fine, less pervasive. This powder is produced by fine handiwork.'

'Cabinet work, for instance?'

'Possibly. I'm not sure. It's even finer than that, in my opinion, but before I commit myself I'd like to have a word with the laboratory chief tomorrow.'

Without waiting to hear the end, Janvier had picked up a volume of Bottin's Directory and was busy studying all the addresses in the Rue de Turenne.

This yielded a list of all sorts of trades, some of them surprising, but by some chance nearly all connected with metals or cardboard.

'I thought I'd just mention it to you. I don't know whether it will help.'

Neither did Maigret. In a case like this, one never knows what may help. At all events this tended to support the testimony of Frans Steuvels, who had always denied being the owner of the blue suit.

But then why did he own a blue overcoat, that went so badly with a brown suit?

Telephone! Sometimes six instruments would be in use at the same time, and the switchboard operator was going out of his mind, for there were not enough people to take all the calls.

'What is it?'

'Lagny.'

Maigret had been there once. It's a little town on the edge of the Marne, with a lot of men fishing and shiny canoes. He couldn't remember the case he had been on down there, but it was in summer, and he had drunk a light white wine, the memory of which still lingered.

Lucas was taking notes, indicating to the chief-inspector that this seemed important.

'Maybe we've got hold of something,' he sighed as he hung up. 'That was the Lagny police station. For over a month they've been quite excited down there about a car that fell in the Marne.'

'It fell into the Marne a month ago?'

'As far as I could make out, yes. The sergeant I had on the phone was so anxious to explain and go into detail that in the end I couldn't follow a thing. Besides, he kept dropping names of people I didn't know, as if they were as famous as Jesus Christ or Pasteur, and continually going on about Old Mother Hébart or Hobart, who gets drunk every night, but who is apparently incapable of making anything up.

'To cut it short, about a month ago . . .'

'Did he tell you the exact date?'

'February 15.'

Maigret, very proud at finding a use for it, consulted the list he had just drawn up.

> *February 15 – Countess Panetti and Gloria leave Claridge's at seven o'clock in the evening in Krynker's car.*

'I thought of that. This looks important, you'll see. Well, this old woman, who lives in an isolated house at the edge of the river and hires out canoes to fishermen in summer, went down to the inn for a drink, as she does every evening. When she was returning home she claims that she heard a terrific noise in the darkness and that she's sure it was the noise of a car falling into the Marne.

'The river was in spate at the time. A lane leading from the main road ends at the water's edge, and the mud must have made it slippery.'

'Did she report it to the police straight away?'

'She talked about it in the café next day. It took some time to get around. It finally reached the ears of a policeman, who questioned her.

'The policeman went down for a look, but the banks were partly submerged, and the current was so violent that navigation had to be suspended for a couple of weeks. Apparently the level is only just now getting back to normal.

'I think the truth is that they didn't take the whole matter very seriously.

'Yesterday, after receiving our alert about the chocolate-coloured car, they had a phone call from someone who lives at the corner of the main road and the lane in question and claims that last month he saw, in the darkness, a car of that colour turning outside his house.

'He's a petrol station proprietor who was filling up a customer's car, which explains why he was outside at that time.'

'What time?'

'Just after nine o'clock at night.'

It doesn't take two hours to get from the Champs-Élysées to Lagny, but of course there was nothing to prevent Krynker from making a detour.

'And so?'

'The police applied to the Ministry of Transport for a crane.'

'Yesterday?'

'Yesterday afternoon. There was a crowd watching it work. Anyhow in the evening they caught something, but the darkness prevented them from carrying on. They even told me the name of the hole, because all the river holes are well known to the fishermen and local people; there's one that's thirty feet deep.'

'Did they fish the car out?'

'This morning. It is in fact a Chrysler, chocolate-coloured, with an Alpes-Maritimes registration number. That's not all. There's a body inside.'

'Male?'

'Female. It's terribly decomposed. Most of the clothing's been torn off by the current. It's got long grey hair.'

'The countess?'

'I don't know. They've only just discovered it. The corpse is still on the bank, under a tarpaulin, and they want to know what they're to do with it. I said I'd ring them back.'

Moers had left a few minutes too soon, for he was the man who would have been invaluable to the chief-inspector, and there wasn't much chance of finding him at home.

'Would you call Dr Paul?'

The latter answered in person.

'You're not busy? You've no plans for the day? Would it be too inconvenient if I came over and picked you up to take you to Lagny? With your bag, yes. No. It won't be a pretty sight. An old woman who's spent a month in the Marne.'

Maigret looked around and saw Lapointe glance away, blushing. The young man was obviously burning with the desire to accompany the chief.

'You haven't got a date with a girl for this afternoon?'

'Oh no, chief-inspector.'

'Can you drive?'

'I've had my licence for two years.'

'Go and fetch the blue Peugeot and wait for me downstairs. Make sure there's enough petrol.'

And to Janvier, disappointed:

'You take another car and drive down slowly, questioning the garage men, innkeepers, anyone you like. It's possible that somebody else may have noticed the chocolate-coloured car. I'll see you at Lagny.'

He drank the spare glass of beer, and a few minutes later Dr Paul's cheerful beard was settling itself in the car with Lapointe proudly at the wheel.

'Shall I take the shortest way?'

'Preferably, young man.'

It was one of the first fine days, and there were a lot of

cars on the road, with families and picnic baskets piled inside.

Dr Paul told stories of post-mortems which, from his lips, became as funny as Jewish stories or ones about lunatics.

At Lagny they had to ask the way, drive out of the little town, make some long detours before arriving at a bend in the river where a crane was surrounded by at least a hundred people. The police were having as much trouble as on fair days. An officer was on the scene and seemed relieved to see the chief-inspector.

The chocolate-coloured car, covered with mud, grass and scarcely identifiable flotsam, was there, upside down on the bank, with water still dripping from all its cracks. Its chassis was battered, one of the windows broken, both headlights smashed, but by an extraordinary chance one door was still functioning, through which they had removed the corpse.

The latter, under the tarpaulin, formed a little heap which no sightseer could approach without a feeling of nausea.

'I'll leave you to it, doctor.'

'Here?'

Dr Paul would have been willing to do it. With his eternal cigarette in his mouth, he had been known to carry out post-mortems in the most unlikely places, and even to break off and remove his rubber gloves in order to eat a snack.

'Can you take the body to the police station, officer?'

'My men will see to it. Stand back, everybody. And the children! Who's letting children come so close?'

Maigret was examining the car when an old woman plucked him by the sleeve and said proudly:

'It was me who found it.'

'Are you Widow Hébart?'

'Hubart, sir. That's my house that you can see behind the ash trees.'

'Tell me what you saw.'

'I didn't see anything actually, but I heard. I was coming back along the tow-path. That's the path we're on.'

'Had you had a lot to drink?'

'Only two or three little glasses.'

'Where were you?'

'Fifty yards from here, further on, towards my house. I heard a car coming in from the main road and I said to myself it must be poachers again. Because it was too cold for lovers, and it was raining into the bargain. All I saw, when I turned round, was the beam from the headlights.

'I wasn't to know that this was going to be important some day, was I? I kept on walking and I had the impression that the car had stopped.'

'Because you couldn't hear the engine any more?'

'Yes.'

'You had your back to the lane?'

'Yes. Then I heard the engine again and I thought the car was turning round. Not a bit of it! Immediately afterwards there was a big splash, and when I looked round the car was gone.'

'You didn't hear any screams?'

'No.'

'You didn't retrace your steps?'

'Should I have? What could I have done all by myself? It had upset me. I thought the poor people had been drowned and I hurried home to get a drink to revive me.'

'You didn't stay by the water's edge?'

'No, sir.'

'You didn't hear anything after the splash?'

'I thought I heard something, like footsteps, but I decided it must be a rabbit frightened by the noise.'

'Is that all?'

'Don't you think it's enough? If they'd listened to me instead of treating me like a crazy old woman, the lady would have been out of the water long ago. Have you seen her?'

Not without a grimace of disgust, Maigret imagined this old woman contemplating the other decomposed old woman.

Did Widow Hubart realize that it was a miracle she was still alive and that if her curiosity had impelled her to turn back on that notable evening she would probably have followed the other woman into the Marne?

'Won't the reporters be coming?'

That's what she was waiting for, to have her picture in the papers.

Lapointe, covered with mud, was climbing out of the Chrysler, which he had examined.

'I didn't find a thing,' he said. 'The tools are in their place in the boot, with the spare tyre. There's no luggage, no handbag. There was only a woman's shoe caught in the back of the seat, and in the dashboard cupboard this pair of gloves and this electric torch.'

The pigskin gloves were a man's, so far as one could tell.

'Go over to the railway station. Someone must have taken a train that night. Unless there are any taxis in the town. Meet me at the police station.'

He preferred to wait in the courtyard, smoking his pipe, until Dr Paul, installed in the garage, had finished his task.

Chapter Eight

'Are you disappointed, Monsieur Maigret?'

Young Lapointe was longing to say 'Chief', like Lucas, Torrence and most of the rest of the team, but he felt too much of a newcomer for that; it seemed to him that this was a privilege he would have to earn, like winning one's spurs.

They had just driven Dr Paul home and were on their way back to the Quai des Orfèvres, in a Paris which seemed to them more luminous after the hours spent floundering in the darkness of Lagny. From the Pont Saint-Michel, Maigret could see the light in his own office.

'I'm not disappointed. I wasn't expecting the railway employees to remember passengers whose tickets they punched a month ago.'

'I was wondering what you had in mind.'

He replied quite naturally:

'The suitcase.'

'I swear it was in the workshop the first time I went to the bookbinder's.'

'I don't doubt it.'

'I'm positive it wasn't the suitcase that Sergeant Lucas found that afternoon in the basement.'

'I don't doubt that either. Leave the car in the yard and come up.'

From the animation of the few men on duty it was clear that

something had happened, and Lucas, hearing Maigret come back, hastily opened his office door.

'Some information on Moss, Chief. A girl and her father came in earlier. They wanted to speak to you personally, but after waiting almost two hours they decided to give me the message. She was a pretty girl of sixteen or seventeen, plump and pink-faced, who looks you frankly in the eye. The father's a sculptor who, if I got it straight, once won the Prix de Rome. There's another girl a bit older and a mother. They live on the Boulevard Pasteur, where they manufacture toys. If I'm not mistaken, the young lady came along with her father to prevent him from having a drink on the way, which seems to be his besetting sin. He wears a big black hat and a cravat. Moss, under the name of Peeters, has been living in their house for the last few months.'

'Is he still there?'

'If he were, I'd already have sent some detectives over to arrest him, or rather I'd have gone myself. He left them on March 12.'

'In other words, the day Levine, Gloria and the child disappeared from circulation after the scene in the Place d'Anvers garden.'

'He didn't tell them he was leaving. He went out in the morning as usual and hasn't set foot in the flat again since. I thought you'd prefer to interrogate them yourself. Oh, and something else. Philippe Liotard has telephoned twice already.'

'What does he want?'

'To speak to you. He asked if you'd ring him at the "Chope du Nègre" if you came in before eleven tonight.'

A restaurant which Maigret knew, on the Boulevard Bonne-Nouvelle.

'Get me the "Chope"!'

It was the cashier who answered. She sent someone to fetch the lawyer.

'Is that you, chief-inspector? I expect you must be swamped with work. Have you found him?'

'Who?'

'Moss. I went to the pictures this afternoon and I caught on. Don't you think an informal tête-à-tête might be useful to us both?'

It happened quite by chance. A little earlier, in the car, Maigret had been thinking about the suitcase. And then, while Liotard was talking to him, little Lapointe was entering the office.

'Are you with friends?' the chief-inspector asked Liotard.

'It doesn't matter. When you get here, I'll leave them.'

'Your lady friend?'

'Yes.'

'No one else?'

'Somebody you're not very fond of, I don't know why, which upsets him a good deal.'

That was Alfonsi. They must have made up a foursome again, the two men and their girls.

'Will you have the patience to wait for me if I'm a bit late?'

'I'll wait as long as you like. It's Sunday.'

'Tell Alfonsi I'd like to see him too.'

'He'll be delighted.'

'See you soon.'

He went and closed the two doors of his office, telling Lapointe, who was tactfully about to leave, to stay.

'Come here. Sit down. You want to get ahead in the police, don't you?'

'More than anything else.'

'You made the stupid mistake of talking too much the first day, and this has had consequences which you don't even suspect yet.'

'I'm sorry. I felt so sure of my sister.'

'Do you want to try something difficult? Just a moment. Don't be in too much of a hurry to answer. It's not a matter of a glorious stunt that will get you your name in the papers. Quite the contrary. If you succeed, nobody but we two will ever know about it. If you mess it up, I shall be obliged to disclaim all responsibility for you and maintain that you were acting under your own steam outside my orders.'

'I understand.'

'You don't understand one little bit, but that doesn't matter. If I were to take the job on myself and fail, the whole of the police force would be involved. You're new enough in the building to get away with it.'

Lapointe could not contain his impatience.

'Maître Liotard and Alfonsi are at the "Chope du Nègre" at the moment, where they're waiting for me.'

'Are you going to join them?'

'Not straight away. First I want to make a call in the Boulevard Pasteur, and I'm sure they won't budge from the restaurant before I get there. Suppose I go and join them in an hour at the earliest. It's nine o'clock. You know where the lawyer lives, on the Rue Bergère? It's on the third floor, to the left. As a number of young ladies live in the house, the concierge probably doesn't pay too much attention to who comes and goes.'

'You want me to . . .'

'Yes. You've been taught how to open a door. It won't matter if you leave marks. Quite the contrary. No sense in going through drawers and papers. You're to make sure of just one thing: that the suitcase isn't there.'

'I never thought of that.'

'All right. It's possible and even probable that it isn't there, because Liotard is a cautious chap. That's why you mustn't waste any time. From the Rue Bergère, you're to go straight over to the Rue de Douai, where Alfonsi has Room 33 in the Hôtel du Massif Central.'

'I know.'

'Do the same thing there. The suitcase. Nothing else. Ring me as soon as you've finished.'

'Can I leave now?'

'Go out into the corridor first. I'm going to lock my door and you try to open it. Ask Lucas for the tools.'

Lapointe didn't do too badly and a few minutes later he was hurrying out, utterly overjoyed.

Maigret went in to the inspectors.

'Are you free, Janvier?'

The telephones were still ringing, but, because of the time of night, with less virulence.

'I was giving Lucas a hand, but . . .'

They went downstairs together, and it was Janvier who took the wheel of the little Headquarters car. A quarter of an hour later they reached the quietest, least brightly lit stretch of the Boulevard Pasteur, which, in the peace of a beautiful Sunday evening, seemed like the main avenue of some small town.

'Come up with me.'

They asked for the sculptor, whose name was Grossot, and were directed to the sixth floor. The building was old but very well kept, probably inhabited by civil servants. When they knocked at the door of the sixth-floor flat, the sound of an argument suddenly ceased, and a young girl with full cheeks opened the door, stepped back.

'Was it you who came to my office earlier?'

'That was my sister. Chief-inspector Maigret? Come in. Pay no attention to the mess. We're only just finishing dinner.'

She led them into a huge studio, with sloping ceiling, partly glass, through which the stars could be seen. There were the remains of some cold meat on a long deal table, with an open litre of wine; another girl, who looked like the twin of the one who had opened the door, was tidying her hair with a furtive movement, while a man in a velvet jacket approached the visitors with exaggerated solemnity.

'Welcome to my modest abode, Monsieur Maigret. I hope you will do me the honour of taking a drink with me.'

Since leaving Headquarters the old sculptor must have managed to get something to drink besides the wine at his meal, because his pronunciation was slurred, his gait unsteady.

'Don't pay any attention,' interposed one of the girls. 'He's got himself in a state again.'

She said this without rancour, and the look she gave her father was affectionate, almost motherly.

In the darkest corners of the great room, pieces of sculpture could be vaguely made out, and it was clear that they had been there for a long time.

More recent, part of their present life, were the carved wooden toys lying around on the furniture and filling the room with a good smell of fresh wood.

'When art no longer offers a living to a man and his family,' Grossot was declaiming, 'there's nothing to be ashamed of, is there, in looking to commerce for one's daily bread?'

Madame Grossot appeared; she must have gone to tidy up when she heard the bell. She was a thin woman, sad, with constantly watchful eyes, who must always be foreseeing misfortunes.

'Won't you give the chief-inspector and this gentleman a chair, Hélène?'

'The chief-inspector knows perfectly well that he can make himself at home here, Mother. Don't you, Monsieur Maigret?'

'Didn't you offer him anything?'

'Would you like a glass of wine? There's nothing else in the house on account of Papa.'

She seemed to be the one who controlled the family, at all events the one who was taking control of the conversation.

'We went to the pictures yesterday, near here, and we recognized the man you're looking for. He was using the name Peeters, not Moss. The reason we didn't come to see you earlier was that Papa hesitated to betray him, protesting that he has been our guest and eaten at our table many times.'

'Had he been living here long?'

'About a year. The flat takes up the whole floor. My parents have lived here more than thirty years, and I was born here and so was my sister. There are three rooms besides the studio and the kitchen. Last year the toys didn't bring in much, because of the crisis, and we decided to take a lodger. We put an advertisement in the paper.

'That's how we got to know Monsieur Peeters.'

'What did he say his profession was?'

'He told us that he represented a big English manufacturing firm, that he had his own clients, so there was no need for him to go out much. Sometimes he'd spend the whole day at home and come and give us a hand, in his shirt-sleeves. You see, we all work on the toys, for which my father makes the models. Last Christmas we got an order from the Printemps and we worked night and day.'

Grossot was eyeing the half-empty wine bottle so pathetically that Maigret said to him:

'Very well, pour me half a glass, just to have a drink with you.'

He received in return a look of gratitude, while the girl continued, without taking her eye off her father to be sure he didn't help himself too freely:

'He usually went out towards the end of the afternoon and he would sometimes come home quite late. Occasionally he would take his sample case with him.'

'Did he leave his luggage here?'

'He left his big trunk.'

'Not his suitcase?'

'No. By the way, Olga, did he have his suitcase when he left?'

'No. He didn't bring it back last time he took it out with him.'

'What kind of man was he?'

'He was quiet, very gentle, perhaps rather sad. Sometimes he would stay shut up in his room for hours at a time, and in the end we'd go and ask if he was ill. Other times he'd have breakfast with us and help us all day.

'Occasionally he would disappear for several days and he'd told us beforehand not to worry about him.'

'What did you call him?'

'Monsieur Jean. He called us by our Christian names, except my mother, of course. He would sometimes bring us chocolates, little presents.'

'Never expensive presents?'

'We wouldn't have accepted them.'

'He never had visitors?'

'Nobody ever came. He never got any letters either. I was surprised that a business representative shouldn't receive any letters, and he explained to me that he had a partner in town, with an office, and his correspondence was addressed there.'

'He never seemed odd to you?'

At this she glanced around, murmured casually:

'Well, here, you know!'

'Your health, Monsieur Maigret. To your investigation! As you can see, I no longer count for anything, not only in the domain of art but even in my own house. I don't protest. I say nothing. They're very nice, but for a man who . . .'

'Let the chief inspector talk, Papa.'

'You see?'

'You don't know when your lodger went out with his suit-case for the last time?'

It was Olga, the older girl, who answered:

'The last Saturday before . . .'

She debated whether she ought to continue.

'Before what?'

The younger child reassumed control of the interview.

'Don't blush, Olga. We're always teasing my sister because she had a crush on Monsieur Jean. He wasn't the right age for her and he wasn't handsome, but . . .'

'What about yourself?'

'Never mind that, Olga. One Saturday, about six o'clock, he went out with his suitcase, which was surprising in itself because it was usually on Mondays that he took it with him.'

'Monday afternoons?'

'Yes. We weren't expecting him back, thinking he was going away for the weekend somewhere, and we were making fun of Olga who was moping.'

'That's not true.'

'We haven't the slightest idea what time he came home. Usually we'd hear him open the door. On the Sunday morning we thought his room was empty, and we were just talking about him when he came out, looking ill, and asked my father if he would mind getting him a bottle of brandy. He said he'd caught a cold. He stayed in bed part of the day. Olga, who did his room, noticed that the suitcase wasn't there. She noticed something else, at least she claims she did.'

'I'm sure of it.'

'You may be right. You used to look at him more closely than we did.'

'I'm sure his suit wasn't the same one. It was a blue suit too, but not his, and when he had it on I noticed that it was a bit too big on the shoulders.'

'He didn't say anything about it?'

'No. We didn't mention it either. After that he complained he had got flu and stayed at home for a whole week without going out.'

'Did he read the papers?'

'The morning and evening paper, just as we do.'

'You didn't notice anything out of the ordinary?'

'No. Except that he'd go and shut himself up in his room the minute anybody knocked at the door.'

'When did he start going out again?'

'About a week later. The last time he slept here was the night of March 11. That's easy to be sure of because on the calendar in his room the leaves haven't been torn off since then.'

'What ought we to do, chief-inspector?' asked the mother anxiously. 'Do you think he's really committed a crime?'

'I don't know, madame.'

'If the police are looking for him . . .'

'May we have a look at his room?'

It was at the end of a passage. Spacious, not luxurious, but clean, with old polished furniture and reproductions of Michelangelo on the walls. An enormous black trunk, of the most common kind, was in the right-hand corner, tied up with cord.

'Open it, please, Janvier.'

'Shall I go out?' asked the girl.

He didn't see any necessity. Janvier had more trouble with the cord than with the lock, which was simple. A strong smell of mothballs pervaded the room, and suits, shoes, underwear began to pile up on the bed.

It might have been an actor's wardrobe, judging by the range of quality and origin in the clothing. A set of tails and a dinner jacket bore the label of a big London tailor, and another dress suit had been made in Milan.

There were also some white linen suits of the kind worn mainly in the tropics, some pretty loud outfits, others which, on the contrary, might have belonged to a bank clerk, and for all of them there were matching shoes, bought in Paris, Nice, Brussels, Rotterdam or Berlin.

Finally, at the very bottom, separated from the rest by a sheet of brown paper, they unearthed a clown's costume, which the girl stared at in more bewilderment than all the rest.

'Was he an actor?'

'In his own way.'

There was nothing else revealing in the room. The blue suit they had just been talking about wasn't there, for Peeters-Moss was wearing it when he left; perhaps he was still wearing it.

In the drawers, small objects, cigarette cases, wallets, cuff links and collars, keys, a broken pipe, but not a single document, no address book.

'Thank you, mademoiselle. It was very sensible of you to inform us and I'm sure you won't regret it. I suppose you haven't a telephone?'

'We used to have one a few years ago, but . . .'

And in a low voice:

'Papa hasn't always been like this. That's why we can't hold it against him. He used not to drink at all. Then he met some old friends from the Beaux Arts who are just about in the same boat, and he got into the habit of going out with them to a little café in the Saint-Germain area. It didn't do them any good.'

A bench in the studio held several precision tools, for sawing, filing, planing the sometimes minute pieces of wood from which they made cunning toys.

'Take along a bit of sawdust in a paper, Janvier.'

That would please Moers. It was amusing to think that through his analysis alone they would inevitably have made their way in the end to this flat perched high in a building on the Boulevard Pasteur. That would have taken weeks, possibly months, but they would have got there just the same.

It was ten o'clock. The wine bottle was empty, and Grossot proposed to accompany 'these gentlemen' down to the street, which he was not permitted to do.

'I'll probably be back.'

'What about him?'

'I don't expect so. In any case I don't think you have anything at all to fear from him.'

'Where shall I drop you, Chief?' asked Janvier, taking the wheel of the car.

'Boulevard Bonne-Nouvelle. Not too near the "Chope du Nègre". Wait for me.'

It was one of those big restaurants that serve sauerkraut and frankfurters, where on Saturday and Sunday evenings four half-starved musicians play on a dais. Maigret immediately spied the two couples not far from the front window, noted that the two ladies had ordered green crème de menthes.

Alfonsi was the first to stand up, not completely sure of himself, like a man who expects a kick in the pants, while the lawyer, smiling, self-possessed, held out his well-kept hand.

'May I introduce our lady friends?'

He did so condescendingly.

'Would you like to sit down for a minute at this table or do you want to move over to a separate one right away?'

'On condition that Alfonsi keeps the ladies company and waits for me, I'd rather hear what you have to say now.'

A table was vacant near the cash desk. The clientele was mainly made up of local shopkeepers treating their families to dinner in a restaurant, just as Maigret had done the night before. There were also some regular customers, bachelors or unhappily married men, playing cards or chess.

'What will you have? A beer? One beer and one brandy and water, waiter.'

It would probably not be long before Liotard was frequenting bars near the Opéra and the Champs-Élysées, but for the present he still felt more at home in this neighbourhood where he could stare at people with an air of great superiority.

'Has your alert brought any results?'

'Was it to question me, Maître Liotard, that you invited me to come and see you?'

'Maybe it was to make peace. What would you say to that? Perhaps I was a bit short with you. Don't forget that we're on opposite sides of the fence. Your job is to destroy my client, mine is to save him.'

'Even by becoming his accomplice?'

The shot went home. The young lawyer with the long, pinched nostrils blinked two or three times.

'I don't know what you mean. But since you prefer it, I'll come straight to the point. As luck would have it, chief-inspector, you're in a position to do me a lot of harm, even to delay, if not interrupt, a career which everyone agrees will be brilliant.'

'I don't doubt it.'

'Thank you. The Bar Council is pretty strict about certain rules, and I admit that in my hurry to get ahead I haven't always stuck to them.'

Maigret was drinking his beer with the most innocent air in the world, watching the cashier, and she might have mistaken him for the hat-maker from the shop round the corner.

'I'm waiting, Maître Liotard.'

'I hoped you might help me, because you know very well what I'm referring to.'

He still did not react.

'You know, chief-inspector, I come from a poor family, very poor . . .'

'The Counts de Liotard?'

'I said very poor, not plebeian. I had a hard time paying my way through the university and when I was a student I had to take all kinds of jobs. I even wore a uniform in a big cinema on the Grands Boulevards.'

'Congratulations.'

'Only a month ago I wasn't eating every day. I was waiting, like all my colleagues of my own age, and some older ones too, for a case that would give me a chance to distinguish myself.'

'You've found it.'

'I've found it. That's what I'm getting at. On Friday, in Monsieur Dossin's office, you uttered certain words which made me think that you knew a great deal about this business and that you wouldn't hesitate to use it against me.'

'Against you?'

'Against my client, if you prefer.'

'I don't understand.'

Of his own accord he ordered another beer, for he had rarely drunk any as good, especially in contrast to the sculptor's lukewarm wine. He was still watching the cashier, as if he was glad she looked so much like the old-fashioned café cashiers, with her big bust pushed up by her corset, her black silk blouse ornamented with a cameo, her hair like a set-piece in a hairdresser's window.

'You were saying?'

'Very well then. You're determined to make me come clean and you've got the whip hand. I made a professional error in soliciting Steuvels to become my client.'

'Only one?'

'I happened to hear about the whole thing in a perfectly

casual way and I hope no one is going to have any trouble on my account. I'm quite friendly with a certain Antoine Bizard; we live in the same building. We've been through the mill together. We've been reduced to sharing a tin of sardines or a camembert. Recently Bizard got a steady job on a paper. He has a girl friend.'

'The sister of one of my detectives.'

'So you do know.'

'I like hearing you tell it.'

'Through his job on the paper, for which he does miscellaneous items, Bizard is in a position to hear about certain matters before they become public . . .'

'Crimes, for instance.'

'If you like. He's got into the habit of phoning me.'

'So that you can go and offer your services?'

'You're a cruel winner, Monsieur Maigret.'

'Go on.'

He was still looking at the cashier and at the same time making sure that Alfonsi was keeping the two women company.

'I was informed that the police were interested in a bookbinder in the Rue de Turenne.'

'On February 21, early in the afternoon.'

'That's right. I went over there and I really did talk about an *ex libris* before bringing up a hotter matter.'

'The furnace.'

'That's all. I told Steuvels that if he was in any trouble I'd be glad to defend him. You know all that. And it was not so much for my own sake that I instigated the conversation we've had tonight, which I hope will remain strictly between the two of us, as for my client's. Anything that would harm me at the moment would harm him by repercussion. There it is, Monsieur Maigret. It's for you to decide. I may be suspended from the Bar tomorrow morning. All you have to do is go and see the President and tell him what you know.'

'Did you stay at the bookbinder's long?'

'Fifteen minutes at the most.'

'Did you see his wife?'

'I think at one point she stuck her head out of the staircase.'

'Did Steuvels take you into his confidence?'

'No. I'm prepared to give you my word of honour on that.'

'One more question, Maître. How long has Alfonsi been working for you?'

'He's not working for me. He's running a private detective agency.'

'Of which he's the only employee!'

'That's none of my business. To defend my client with any chance of success I need certain information which it would be unbecoming for me to dig up for myself.'

'Primarily you needed to be kept up to date on what I know.'

'That's fair enough, isn't it?'

The cashier was picking up the telephone, which had just rung, and answering:

'Just a minute. I don't know. I'll find out.'

As she was opening her mouth to give a name to the waiter, the chief-inspector stood up.

'Is it for me?'

'What's your name?'

'Maigret.'

'Do you want to take it in the booth?'

'Never mind. I'll only be a second.'

It was the call he was expecting from young Lapointe. The latter's voice was tense with excitement.

'Is that you, chief-inspector? *I've got it!*'

'Where?'

'I didn't find anything at the lawyer's, where I nearly got

caught by the concierge. I went over to the Rue de Douai as you had told me. There are crowds of people going in and out there. It was easy. I had no trouble opening the door. The suitcase was under the bed. What shall I do with it?'

'Where are you?'

'At the tobacconist's on the corner of the Rue de Douai.'

'Take a taxi to the Quai. I'll meet you there.'

'Yes, chief. Are you pleased?'

Carried away by his enthusiasm and pride, he had ventured to use the 'word' for the first time . . . though not with complete confidence . . .

'You've done a good job.'

The lawyer was watching Maigret uneasily. The chief-inspector sat down again at his place on the bench with a sigh of satisfaction, signalled to the waiter.

'Another beer. Perhaps you'd be good enough to bring this gentleman a brandy.'

'But . . .'

'Pipe down, boy.'

That made the lawyer gasp.

'Look, it's not the Bar Council I'm going to report you to. It's the Public Prosecutor. Tomorrow morning I'll probably ask him for two warrants for arrest, one in your name, and one in that of your pal Alfonsi.'

'Are you serious?'

'What's that likely to get you, suppression of evidence in a murder case? I'll have to look up the statute book. I'll think it over. May I leave the bill to you?'

Already on his feet, he added softly, confidentially, leaning over Philippe Liotard's shoulder:

'I've got the suitcase!'

Chapter Nine

Maigret had rung the judge's office the first time at about half past nine and spoken to the clerk:

'Would you ask Monsieur Dossin if he can see me?'

'Here he is now.'

'Something new?' the judge had asked. 'I mean besides what's in the morning press?'

He was very excited. The papers reported the discovery of the chocolate-coloured car and the corpse of the old woman at Lagny.

'I think so. I'll come and tell you about it.'

But since then, every time the chief-inspector was making for the door of his office something would delay him, a telephone call, or the arrival of a detective who had a report to make. The judge had called back discreetly, asked Lucas:

'Is the chief-inspector still there?'

'Yes. Shall I put him on?'

'No. I suppose he's busy. I'm sure he'll be up in a minute.'

At a quarter past ten he had finally made up his mind to get Maigret on the line.

'Sorry to bother you. I imagine you're swamped. But I'm having Frans Steuvels brought in at eleven o'clock and I wouldn't want to begin the interrogation before seeing you.'

'Would you mind if your interrogation turned into a confrontation?'

'Who with?'

'With his wife, probably. If I may, I'll get a detective to fetch her just on the chance.'

'Do you want an official summons?'

'That won't be necessary.'

Monsieur Dossin waited a good ten minutes more, pretending to study the dossier. At last there was a knock at the door, he almost made a rush to open it and saw Maigret silhouetted, a suitcase in his hand.

'Are you going away?'

The chief-inspector's smile enlightened him, and he murmured, not able to believe his eyes:

'The suitcase?'

'It's heavy, I can tell you.'

'So we were right?'

He was relieved of a great weight. The systematic campaign of Philippe Liotard had finally shaken him and it was he, after all, who had taken the responsibility of keeping Steuvels in prison.

'Is he guilty?'

'Guilty enough to be put inside for several years.'

Maigret had known the contents of the suitcase since the previous evening, but he made the inventory again, with all the pleasure of a child setting out his Christmas presents.

What made the brown suitcase, with its handle mended with string, so heavy, were some pieces of metal which looked a bit like bookbinder's stamps, but which were actually the seals of various sovereign states.

Conspicuous among them were those of the United States and of all the South American republics.

There were also some rubber stamps like those used in town halls and government offices, all arranged as carefully as a commercial traveller's samples.

'This is Steuvels's work,' explained Maigret. 'His brother

Alfred provided him with the models and the blank passports. As far as I can tell from these specimens, the passports weren't counterfeit but were obtained by thefts from consulates.'

'Had they been in this racket long?'

'I don't think so. Two years roughly, judging by the bank accounts. In fact this morning I telephoned most of the banks in Paris, and that's partly what kept me from coming up to see you earlier.'

'Steuvels has an account at the Société Générale in the Rue Saint-Antoine, hasn't he?'

'He has another in an American bank in the Place Vendôme, another in an English bank on the Boulevard. So far we've found five different accounts. It began two years ago, which corresponds with the date when his brother came back to Paris to live.'

It was raining. The weather was grey and mild. Maigret was sitting by the window, smoking his pipe.

'You see, Monsieur le Juge, Alfred Moss doesn't fall into the category of professional criminals. Those men have one speciality and most of the time they stick to it. I've never known a pickpocket turn burglar, nor a burglar forge cheques or try confidence tricking.

'Alfred Moss is a clown, first and foremost, an acrobat.

'It was as a result of a fall that he got into the game. If I'm not much mistaken, he brought off his first job by chance when, cashing in on his knowledge of languages, he was taken on by a big London hotel as an interpreter. An opportunity arose to steal some jewellery, and he seized it.

'This was enough for him to live on for a time. Not for long, because he has one vice; I found this out this morning too, from his local bookie: he bets on the races.

'Like any amateur, he didn't stick to one type of theft, but wanted to try everything.

'He did it with unusual skill and luck, since it's never been possible to prove anything against him.

'He had his ups and downs. A confidence trick would follow some forged cheques.

'He wasn't as young as he used to be, was known to the police in most capitals, blacklisted in the big hotels where he had usually operated.'

'That's when he remembered his brother?'

'Yes. Two years ago, the gold traffic, which had been his previous activity, wasn't paying off any more. On the other hand, faked passports, especially for America, were beginning to bring astronomical prices. He reasoned that a bookbinder, accustomed to reproducing coats of arms on little blocks, would be able to do just as good a job with official seals.'

'What amazes me is that Steuvels, who doesn't lack for anything, should have accepted. Unless he leads a double life which we haven't discovered.'

'He doesn't lead a double life. Poverty, real poverty of the kind he knew in his childhood and adolescence, produces two kinds of people: the extravagant and the miserly. It more often produces misers, and they're so afraid of seeing the bad days return that they're capable of anything at all to provide against them.

'If I'm not greatly mistaken, that's the case with Steuvels. The list of banks where he's made deposits offers additional proof. I'm convinced this wasn't just a way of hiding his nest-egg, because it never occurred to him that he might be found out. But he was suspicious of banks, of nationalizations, devaluations, and he would put by a bit here and a bit there, in different banking houses.'

'I thought he practically never went out without his wife.'

'That's right. It was she who went out without him, and it took me some time to discover that. Every Monday afternoon, she went to the Vert-Galant laundry-barge to do her washing. Almost every Monday Moss would come over with his suit-case, and when he was early, he'd wait at the "Tabac des Vosges" until his sister-in-law had left.

'The two brothers had the afternoon before them for their work. The tools and the compromising documents never remained at the Rue de Turenne. Moss took them away with him.

'On some Mondays, Steuvels would even have time to hurry over to one of his banks and make a deposit.'

'I don't see what part was played by the young woman with the child, or by Countess Panetti, or . . .'

'I'm coming to that, Monsieur le Juge. I told you about the suitcase first because that's what bothered me more than anything else, right from the start. Ever since I knew of the existence of Moss and suspected what he was up to, I've had another question on my mind.

'*Why, on Tuesday, March 12, all of a sudden, when the gang seemed quiet, was there an unusual flare-up which ended in its dispersing?*

'I mean the incident in the Place d'Anvers garden, which my wife happened to witness.

'Only the night before, Moss was living peacefully in his lodgings on the Boulevard Pasteur.

'Levine and the child were staying at the Hôtel Beauséjour, where Gloria would come and pick up the child every morning to take him for a walk.

'Now, on that Tuesday, about ten in the morning, Moss enters the Hôtel Beauséjour, in which, probably as a pre-caution, he has never set foot before.

'Immediately Levine packs his bags, dashes over to the Place d'Anvers, calls Gloria, who deserts the child in order to follow him.

'By the afternoon they've all disappeared, leaving no trace.

'What happened on the morning of March 12?

'Moss couldn't have received a telephone call because the house he lived in has no telephone.

'Neither I nor my detectives made any move at that moment that might have alarmed the gang, the existence of which we didn't even suspect.

'As for Frans Steuvels, he was in the Santé.

'All the same, something did happen.

'And it was only last night, when I went home, that through the wildest chance I found the answer to this question.'

Monsieur Dossin was so relieved to know that the man he had put in prison was not innocent that he was listening with a sort of beatific smile, as if he were hearing a story being told.

'My wife had been waiting for me all evening and had spent the time catching up on a little job she takes care of now and again. This consists of keeping scrap-books of all newspaper clippings that mention me, and she does it more devotedly than ever since a former Director of Police Headquarters published his memoirs.

'"You might possibly write yours some day, after you've retired and we're living in the country," she'll reply when I make fun of her hobby.

'In any case, when I got home last night, the scissors and paste were on the table. While I was making myself comfortable, I happened to glance over my wife's shoulder, and in one of the clippings she was just pasting in I saw a photo which I had completely forgotten.

'It had been taken three years ago by a little newspaperman in Normandy: we were spending a few days at Dieppe, and he'd caught us, my wife and myself, on the steps of our *pension*.

'What amazed me was to see this photo on a page from an illustrated magazine.

' "Didn't you read it? It came out recently: a four-page article on the early days of your career and your methods."

'There were some other photographs, one of me when I was secretary in a police station and had a drooping moustache.

' "What's the date of it?"

' "Of the article? Last week. I haven't had time to show it to you. You've hardly been home lately."

'In short, Monsieur Dossin, the article had appeared in a Paris weekly which went on sale on the morning of Tuesday, March 12.

'I immediately sent someone over to see the people who still had Moss as their lodger on that date, and they confirmed that the younger of the girls had taken the magazine in to him, with the milk, at about half past eight, and that Moss had glanced at it while he was having breakfast.

'From then on, everything's straightforward. This even explains Gloria's long sessions on the garden bench in the Place d'Anvers.

'After their two murders and the arrest of Steuvels, the gang, now broken up, was lying low. Levine probably changed hotels several times before moving into the Rue Lepic. For safety he never appeared with Gloria outside, and they even went so far as to avoid spending the night together in the same place.

'Moss must have come to the Place d'Anvers every morning to keep in touch, and all he had to do was take a seat at the end of the bench.

'Now, as you know, my wife sat down three or four times on that same bench before her dentist's appointment. The two women had got to know each other and would chat. Moss had probably seen Madame Maigret, to whom he hadn't paid any attention.

'Imagine his reaction when he found out from the magazine

that the good lady on the bench was none other than the wife of the chief-inspector in charge of the investigation!

'He couldn't believe it was accidental, could he? He quite naturally thought that we were on his track and that I had turned over this delicate bit of sleuthing to my wife.

'He rushed over to the Rue Lepic and alerted Levine, who dashed over to warn Gloria.'

'Why did they have a quarrel?'

'Perhaps about the child? Perhaps Levine didn't want Gloria to go back for him, thus running the risk of being arrested. She insisted on going, but with maximum precautions.

'This also makes me inclined to think that when we find them again they won't be together. They'll reckon that we know Gloria and the boy, while we know nothing about Levine. He must have gone off in one direction, and Moss in another.'

'Do you expect to catch them?'

'Maybe tomorrow, maybe a year from now. You know how things go.'

'You still haven't told me where you found the suitcase.'

'Perhaps you would prefer not to know *how* we got possession of it? I was, in fact, forced to use slightly illegal methods, for which I take sole responsibility, but you couldn't possibly approve them.

'All you need to know is that it was Liotard who relieved Steuvels of the compromising suitcase.

'For one reason or another, on the Saturday night, Moss had taken the suitcase to the Rue de Turenne and left it there.

'Frans Steuvels had simply shoved it under a table in his workshop, thinking no one would bother about it.

'On February 21 Lapointe invented a pretext to be admitted and searched the place.

'Remember that Steuvels couldn't get in touch with his

brother, or any other member of the gang probably, to let them know what was going on. I have a theory about that.

'He must have wondered how to get rid of the suitcase and was doubtless waiting until after dark to see about it, when Liotard, whom he'd never heard of, turned up.'

'How did Liotard get to know?'

'Through an indiscretion in my department.'

'One of your detectives?'

'I don't blame him for it, and there's not much chance that it will ever happen again. In any case Liotard offered his services, and even went rather beyond what one is entitled to expect from a member of the Bar, since he took away the suitcase.'

'Did you find it at his place?'

'At Alfonsi's; he'd passed it on to him.'

'Let's see where we stand now . . .'

'Nowhere. I mean, we know nothing about the essential thing, that's the two murders. A man was killed in the Rue de Turenne, and previously Countess Panetti was killed in her car, we don't know where. You must have received the report from Dr Paul, who found a bullet in the old lady's cranium.

'However, a small item of information has reached me from Italy. More than a year ago the Krynkers were divorced in Switzerland, since divorce is impossible in Italy. Countess Panetti's daughter regained her liberty to marry an American, with whom she is now living in Texas.'

'There was never a reconciliation with her mother?'

'Far from it. Her mother was more furious with her than ever. Krynker is a Hungarian of good family, but poor. He spent part of the winter at Monte Carlo trying to make his fortune at gambling, without success.

'He arrived in Paris three weeks before the death of his ex-mother-in-law and lived at the Commodore, then in a small hotel on the Rue Caumartin.'

'How long had Gloria Lotti been in the old lady's service?'

'Four or five months. That hasn't been determined exactly.'

A sound was heard in the corridor, and the doorman came to announce that the prisoner had arrived.

'Am I to tell him all this?' asked Monsieur Dossin, whose responsibilities were weighing on him again.

'There are two possibilities: either he'll talk, or he'll still refuse to. I've had dealings with several Flemings in my time, and I've learned that they're hard to soften up. If he won't talk, it will take us weeks or more. We'll have to wait, in fact, until we rout out one of the four characters holed up Lord knows where.'

'Four?'

'Moss, Levine, the woman and the child, and our best bet may be the child.'

'Unless they've got rid of him.'

'If Gloria went back for him when he was in my wife's charge, at the risk of getting herself arrested, she must be attached to him.'

'Do you think it's her son?'

'I'm sure of it. It's a mistake to think criminals aren't like other people, that they can't have children and love them.'

'Her son by Levine?'

'Probably.'

Rising to his feet, Dossin smiled a faint smile with a trace of mischief and of humility too.

'This would be the time for a "grilling", wouldn't it? Unfortunately that's not my strong point.'

'If you'll allow me, I can try talking to Liotard.'

'To get him to advise his client to talk?'

'As matters stand now, it's in the interest of both of them.'

'Shall I have them brought in right away?'

'In a moment.'

Maigret went out and said cordially to the man sitting to the right of the door, on the bench worn smooth by constant use:

'Good morning, Steuvels.'

Just at that moment Janvier was coming out into the corridor, together with a very distressed Fernande. The inspector was doubtful about letting the woman join her husband.

'You have time for a chat together,' Maigret said to them.

'The judge isn't quite ready.'

He made Liotard a sign to follow him, and they talked in undertones, pacing up and down the murky corridor where there were policemen outside most of the doors. It took barely five minutes.

'When you're ready, just knock.'

Maigret went alone into Monsieur Dossin's office, leaving Liotard, Steuvels and Fernande in conversation.

'Satisfactory result?'

'We'll see. Liotard's willing, obviously. I'll cook you up a nice little report in which I'll manage to mention the suitcase without emphasizing it.'

'That's a bit irregular, isn't it?'

'Do you want to catch the murderers?'

'I understand you, Maigret. But my father and my grandfather were on the Bench, and I think I'll end my days there too.'

He was blushing, waiting for a knock on the door with a mixture of impatience and misgiving.

At last it opened.

'Shall I bring Madame Steuvels in too?' asked the lawyer.

Fernande had been crying and had her handkerchief in her hand. She immediately tried to catch Maigret's eye to give him a look of distress, as though she felt confident that he could still put everything right.

Steuvels, for his part, hadn't changed. He was still wearing an expression that was both mild and stubborn at the same time, and he went and sat down obediently on the chair he was motioned to.

As the clerk was about to take his place, Monsieur Dossin said to him:

'Wait. I'll call you when the interrogation becomes official. Are you agreeable, Maître Liotard?'

'Quite. Thank you.'

Maigret was the only one standing up now, facing the window, down which little raindrops were rolling. The Seine was grey like the sky; the barges, the roofs, the pavements reflected the wetness.

Then, after two or three little coughs, Judge Dossin's voice was heard, saying diffidently:

'I believe the chief-inspector would like to put a few questions to you, Steuvels.'

Maigret, who had just lighted his pipe, had no alternative but to turn round, trying to suppress a smile of amusement.

'I suppose,' he began, still standing up, as if he were addressing a class, 'your counsel has briefly given you the picture? We know what you and your brother have been up to. Possibly, so far as you personally are concerned, we may have nothing else to charge you with.

'It was not, in fact, your suit which showed traces of blood, but that of your brother, who left his suit with you and took yours away with him.'

'My brother didn't commit murder either.'

'Probably not. Do you want me to interrogate you, or would you rather tell us what you know?'

Not only was Maître Liotard on his side now, but Fernande, by the look in her eyes, was urging Frans to talk.

'Question me. I'll see if I can answer.'

He wiped the thick lenses of his glasses and waited, round-shouldered, head slightly bent forward as if it were too heavy.

'When did you learn that Countess Panetti had been killed?'

'In the course of Saturday night.'

'You mean the night when Moss, Levine and a third person, who is probably Krynker, came to your house?'

'Yes.'

'Was it your idea to send a telegram to get your wife out of the way?'

'I wasn't even told about it.'

This was plausible. Alfred Moss was sufficiently familiar with the couple's domestic habits and way of life.

'So when someone knocked at your door about nine o'clock that evening you didn't know what it was about?'

'Yes. Anyhow, I didn't want to let them in. I was reading peacefully in the basement.'

'What did your brother tell you?'

'That one of his companions needed a passport that same evening and he'd brought everything along and I'd better get to work.'

'Was that the first time he'd brought strangers to your house?'

'He knew I didn't want to see anyone.'

'But you knew he had accomplices?'

'He'd told me he was working with a man named Schwartz.'

'The man who called himself Levine at the Rue Lepic? A rather fat man, very dark?'

'Yes.'

'You all went down to the basement together?'

'Yes. I couldn't work in the workshop at that time of night, or the neighbours would have wondered what was up.'

'Tell me about the third man.'

'I don't know him.'

'Did he have a foreign accent?'

'Yes. He was a Hungarian. He seemed anxious to get away

and he kept on asking if he wouldn't run into trouble with a false passport.'

'For what country?'

'The United States. They're the hardest to fake because of certain special signs known only to the consuls and the immigration department.'

'So you started work?'

'I didn't have time.'

'What happened?'

'Schwartz was inspecting the flat, as if he was making sure no one could take us by surprise. Suddenly, while I had my back turned – I was bending over the suitcase which was placed on a chair – I heard a shot and saw the Hungarian slumping to the floor.'

'Was it Schwartz who had fired?'

'Yes.'

'Did your brother seem surprised?'

A moment's hesitation.

'Yes.'

'What happened next?'

'Schwartz maintained that this was the only possible way out and that he couldn't help it. According to him, Krynker had lost his nerve and would inevitably have been caught. If he'd been caught, he would have talked.

' "I was wrong to treat him like a man," he added.

'Then he asked me where the furnace was.'

'He knew there was one?'

'I think so.'

Through Moss, obviously, as it was obvious also that Frans did not want to lay it to his brother's charge.

'He ordered Alfred to start a fire and asked me to bring some very sharp tools.

' "We're all in the same boat, boys. If I hadn't shot down this idiot we'd have been arrested within a week. Nobody saw him with us. Nobody knows he's here. He has no family to start making inquiries. Get him out of the way and we'll be all right." '

This wasn't the moment to ask the bookbinder if they had all helped with the dismemberment.

'Did he tell you about the old lady's death?'

'Yes.'

'Was this the first you heard of it?'

'I hadn't seen anybody since the point where they left in the car.'

He was becoming more reticent, while Fernande's glance was travelling from her husband's face to Maigret's.

'Speak out, Frans. They got you into it and then cleared out. What good would it do you to keep quiet?'

Maître Liotard was adding:

'In my capacity as your counsel, I can tell you that it's not only your duty to speak out, but in your own interest too. I think the court will take your frankness into consideration.'

Frans looked at him with big worried eyes and shrugged his shoulders slightly.

'They spent part of the night at my place,' he finally brought out. 'It took a very long time.'

A sudden heave of her stomach made Fernande put her handkerchief to her mouth.

'Schwartz, or Levine, never mind his name, had a bottle of brandy in his overcoat pocket, and my brother drank a lot.

'At one point Schwartz said to him, looking furious:

' "That's the second time you've played this trick on me."

'And that was when Alfred told me the story of the old lady.'

'Just a minute,' interrupted Maigret. 'What exactly do you know about Schwartz?'

'He was the man my brother was working for. He had talked

to me about him several times. He thought he was a fine fellow, but dangerous. He has a child by a pretty girl, an Italian, whom he lives with most of the time.'

'Gloria?'

'Yes. Schwartz worked mainly in the big hotels. He'd got on to a very rich, eccentric woman, whom he expected to get a lot out of, and he'd made Gloria take a job as her maid.'

'And Krynker?'

'I really only saw him dead, because the shot was fired when he'd only been in my house a few minutes. There are some things I didn't understand until later, when I thought about it.'

'For instance?'

'That Schwartz had prepared the whole thing in minute detail. He wanted to get Krynker out of the way and he'd hit upon this method of getting rid of him without running any risk. When he came to my house he knew what was going to happen. He'd made Gloria go to Concarneau to send off the telegram to Fernande.'

'And the old lady?'

'I wasn't mixed up in that business. I only know that since his divorce Krynker, who was on the Riviera, had tried to get in touch with her. Recently he succeeded, and she would sometimes give him small amounts of money. This would immediately melt away, because he liked to lead a grand life. What he wanted was enough money to get to the United States.'

'Was he still in love with his wife?'

'I don't know. He met Schwartz, or rather Schwartz, tipped off by Gloria, managed to meet him in a bar, and they became more or less friendly.'

'Was it on the night of Krynker's death and the furnace that they told you all this?'

'We had to wait hours while . . .'

'We know.'

'I wasn't told whether it was Krynker's idea or whether Schwartz suggested it to him. Apparently the old lady was in the habit of travelling with a case containing jewellery worth a fortune.

'It was about the time of year when she regularly went to the Riviera. It was just a matter of inducing her to go in Krynker's car.

'On the way, at a prearranged point, the car would be attacked and the jewel case stolen.

'In Krynker's mind, this was to be managed without bloodshed. He was convinced that he wasn't running any risk, since he would be in the car with his ex-mother-in-law.

'For some reason or other, Schwartz fired, and I think he did it on purpose because this put the other two at his mercy.'

'Your brother too?'

'Yes.

'The attack took place on the Fontainebleau road, and afterwards they drove as far as Lagny to get rid of the car. Schwartz had a cottage somewhere near there at one time and was familiar with the district. What else do you want to know?'

'Where are the jewels?'

'They found the case all right, but the jewellery wasn't in it. No doubt the countess had her suspicions after all? Gloria, who was with her, knew nothing about it either. Maybe she left them in a bank?'

'That's when Krynker lost his head?'

'He wanted to try to get across the frontier right away, on his own papers, but Schwartz insisted he'd be caught. He couldn't sleep, was drinking a lot. He was bordering on panic, and Schwartz decided that the only way to get any peace at all was to get rid of him. He brought him to my house on the pretext of obtaining a false passport for him.'

'How was it that your brother's suit . . .'

'I understand. At one point Alfred stumbled, exactly where . . .'

'So you gave him your blue suit and kept his, which you cleaned the next day?'

Fernande's head must have been full of bloody pictures. She was looking at her husband as though seeing him for the first time, no doubt trying to imagine him during the days and nights he had then spent alone in the basement and in the workshop.

Maigret saw her shudder, but the next moment she held out a hesitant hand, which finally came to rest on the bookbinder's big paw.

'Perhaps they have a binder's shop at the Big House,' she said, making an effort to smile.

Levine, whose name was neither Schwartz nor Levine, but Sarkistian, and who was wanted by the authorities of three countries, was arrested a month later in a little village near Orléans, where he was spending his time fishing.

Two days later, Gloria Lotti was found in a brothel at Orléans, and she steadfastly refused to reveal the name of the peasants to whom she had entrusted her son.

As for Alfred Moss, his description remained on the police 'Wanted' list for four years.

One night, in a little circus which was travelling from village to village along the roads of the Départment du Nord, a down-at-heel clown hanged himself, and from an examination of the papers found in his suitcase the police discovered his identity.

Countess Panetti's jewels had not left Claridge's, having been locked up in one of the trunks left in the baggage room, and the cobbler in the Rue de Turenne never admitted, not even when he was dead drunk, that it was he who had written the anonymous letter.

PENGUIN RED CLASSICS

LOCK 14
GEORGES SIMENON

'[Simenon's] peculiar accuracy of vision … conveys with such a sure
touch, the bleakness of human life' A. N. Wilson

One rainy night a canal worker stumbles across the strangled body of
Mary Lampson in a stable near Lock 14. The dead woman's husband
seems unmoved by her death and is curt and unhelpful when Maigret
interviews him aboard his yacht. But gradually Maigret is able to piece
together their story – a sordid tale of whisky-filled orgies and nomadic
life on the canals. Can the answer to this crime be found aboard the
yacht? Or is the murderer among the barges, carters and lock-keepers
who work the canal?

In *Lock 14*, Simenon plunges Maigret into the unfamiliar canal world
of shabby bars and shadowy towpaths, drawing together the strands of
a tragic case of lost identity.

For more classic fiction, read Red

www.penguinclassics.com/reds

PENGUIN RED CLASSICS

MAIGRET AND THE GHOST
GEORGES SIMENON

'A novelist who entered his fictional world as if he were part of it'
Peter Ackroyd

Inspector Lognon – a plain-clothes detective with a reputation for
misfortune – is shot in the street with the word 'ghost' on his lips. It
soon emerges that he spent the night in the nearby apartment of a
beautiful young woman, who has since then vanished. While the
injured man fights for his life in hospital, Chief Superintendent Maigret
discovers that the hapless Inspector may finally have been on to
something big. And when he encounters suave art dealer Norris Jonker
and his glamorous wife Mirella, Maigret begins to wonder if their
strange lifestyle is the reason for Lognon's presence on the Avenue
Junot.

In *Maigret and the Ghost*, Simenon's tenacious detective is perplexed
by a constant stream of conflicting evidence as he explores the
underground world of art collecting.

For more classic fiction, read Red

www.penguinclassics.com/reds

PENGUIN RED CLASSICS

MAIGRET IN COURT
GEORGES SIMENON

'A unique teller of tales … What interested Simenon was the average man losing control of his own fate' *Observer*

Dreaming of his retirement to the Loire, Chief Inspector Maigret is dismayed to find himself once again embroiled in a brutal murder case. Gaston Meurant faces the Assizes Court on the charge of killing a small child, but, although the evidence points to his guilt, Maigret doubts that the mild-mannered picture framer can have committed such a horrific crime.

In the tense courtroom drama that ensues, Maigret must expose some unsavoury evidence about the accused man's private life in order to establish the truth and save him from execution, and sees the gentle Meurant turn into an obsessive and vengeful man in a search for justice outside the legal system.

For more classic fiction, read Red

www.penguinclassics.com/reds

PENGUIN RED CLASSICS

THE MAN WHO WATCHED THE TRAINS GO BY
GEORGES SIMENON

'Classic Simenon … extraordinary in its evocative power' *Independent*

Kees Popinga is a quiet clerk in a respectable shipping company. But just before Christmas, the firm goes bust, taking his life savings with it.

And suddenly the mild-mannered family man snaps. He boards a train for Amsterdam and Paris and embarks on a debauched spree. When a prostitute is found murdered, Kees is the prime suspect: a wanted criminal on the run.

Has this model citizen really become a paranoid killer? Or is he just playing a bizarre game of cat and mouse with the policeman who hunts him?

For more classic fiction, read Red

www.penguinclassics.com/reds

PENGUIN RED CLASSICS

THE STRANGERS IN THE HOUSE
GEORGES SIMENON

'A master storyteller … Simenon gave to the puzzle story a humanity that it had never had before' *Daily Telegraph*

Hector Loursat, a lawyer in the town of Moulins, has lived as a drunken recluse since his wife left him eighteen years before. Estranged from society and even his own daughter, he shuts himself in his study, numbed by endless bottles of burgundy. But when a dead man is found in his flat one night, the resulting police investigation unearths secrets that shake the town – and Loursat's seclusion – to the core. No longer able to ignore the outside world, he begins to feel new life running in his veins and emerges to take on the murder case himself.

In the progressive breakdown of Loursat's self-imposed isolation, Simenon brilliantly depicts the psychology of loneliness and a man's tortured re-engagement with humanity and its darkest acts.

For more classic fiction, read Red

www.penguinclassics.com/reds

PENGUIN RED CLASSICS

A MAN'S HEAD
GEORGES SIMENON

'Excellent ... grips from the first line' *Independent*

A rich American widow and her maid have been stabbed to death in a brutal attack. All the evidence points to Joseph, a young drifter, and he is soon arrested. But what is his motive? Or is he just a pawn in a wider conspiracy?

Inspector Maigret believes the police have the wrong man and lets him escape from prison to prove his innocence. Perhaps, with Joseph on the loose, the real murderer will surface.

A deadly game of cross and double-cross has begun ...

'A giant, a genius, a glorious storyteller' *Daily Telegraph*

For more classic fiction, read Red

www.penguinclassics.com/reds

PENGUIN RED CLASSICS

MY FRIEND MAIGRET
GEORGES SIMENON

'The archetypal fictional detective' *Sunday Times*

A small-time crook has been murdered on a Mediterranean island. He
was a nasty piece of work – a drunken thug, pimp and thief. Yet just
before he died he was heard boasting in a crowded bar about his
policeman 'friend' Maigret.

When Inspector Maigret hears about this, he decides to take a little
island holiday to find out what's going on. Nobody there seems to have
a motive for killing Pacaud - not the old English lady and her male
'secretary' nor the ageing prostitute and the Dutch anarchist.

But plenty of them have secrets they'd prefer to keep hidden …

For more classic fiction, read Red
www.penguinclassics.com/reds

PENGUIN RED CLASSICS

THE BAR ON THE SEINE
GEORGES SIMENON

'Simenon was unique … summons up characters – tarts, narks, barmen, witnesses, victims, murderers – like a wizard of life' *Sunday Times*

Inspector Maigret has a nasty job to do. He must visit a prisoner he arrested to tell him he will be executed at dawn. But the condemned man tells Maigret a story about something he saw years before. About a body dumped in a canal. About blackmail. About seeing the murderer again not long ago …

There's probably no point in checking it out now, but the determined policeman still finds himself in a seedy bar to investigate. Is the murderer still one of its regulars? Maigret has a funny feeling about this case …

For more classic fiction, read Red
www.penguinclassics.com/reds

PENGUIN RED CLASSICS

THE FRIEND OF MADAME MAIGRET
GEORGES SIMENON

'A great novelist ... the sheer range of his understanding of the human heart is unparalleled in twentieth-century fiction' Paul Bailey

Maigret becomes increasingly frustrated as his attempts to prove that a brutal, repulsive murder has been committed at a local bookbinder prove fruitless. The mystery revolves around a series of seemingly unconnected incidents and characters, creating an intricate and complicated narrative set amongst the backdrop of the Marais district of Paris.

Eventually it is the intelligent and compassionate Madame Maigret who provides the vital clue ...

For more classic fiction, read Red

www.penguinclassics.com/reds

PENGUIN RED CLASSICS

THE MAN ON THE BOULEVARD
GEORGES SIMENON

'Simenon's Maigret, cool and classic as ever … All mystery buffs should celebrate' Scott Turow

Louis Thouret is found stabbed in an alleyway off the Boulevard Saint-Martin in Paris. His wife seems strangely calm when she identifies the body and is more surprised to see that he is wearing clothes she has never seen before.

As Chief Superintendent Maigret pieces together the dead man's last days, he discovers that Louis had a secret life. He left his job years ago. Somehow he had enough money to convince his conventional wife he was still working. But who would want to kill him? Especially when it seems he just spent his days sitting on a bench on the boulevard, watching the world go by …

For more classic fiction, read Red
www.penguinclassics.com/reds

PENGUIN RED CLASSICS

THE YELLOW DOG
GEORGES SIMENON

'Excellent ... he has given immense pleasure to millions of readers'

Sunday Telegraph

A local wine merchant is shot dead after leaving the Admiral Hotel in the coastal town of Concarneau. When Superintendent Maigret arrives to investigate, he finds the townspeople in a state of panic. One by one, prominent citizens are being attacked. Poison has been discovered in drinks at the hotel bar. The local paper doesn't help matters either, with scaremongering articles asking 'Whose turn next?'

What links the victims? And what is the downtrodden waitress, Emma, hiding from Maigret? As Maigret probes the dark secrets hidden in Concarneau, another mystery arises – why is that strange yellow dog lurking everywhere he turns?

'A supreme writer ... unforgettable vividness' *Independent*

For more classic fiction, read Red

www.penguinclassics.com/reds

He just wanted a decent book to read ...

Not too much to ask, is it? It was in 1935 when Allen Lane, Managing Director of Bodley Head Publishers, stood on a platform at Exeter railway station looking for something good to read on his journey back to London. His choice was limited to popular magazines and poor-quality paperbacks – the same choice faced every day by the vast majority of readers, few of whom could afford hardbacks. Lane's disappointment and subsequent anger at the range of books generally available led him to found a company – and change the world.

'We believed in the existence in this country of a vast reading public for intelligent books at a low price, and staked everything on it'
Sir Allen Lane, 1902–1970, founder of Penguin Books

The quality paperback had arrived – and not just in bookshops. Lane was adamant that his Penguins should appear in chain stores and tobacconists, and should cost no more than a packet of cigarettes.

Reading habits (and cigarette prices) have changed since 1935, but Penguin still believes in publishing the best books for everybody to enjoy. We still believe that good design costs no more than bad design, and we still believe that quality books published passionately and responsibly make the world a better place.

So wherever you see the little bird – whether it's on a piece of prize-winning literary fiction or a celebrity autobiography, political tour de force or historical masterpiece, a serial-killer thriller, reference book, world classic or a piece of pure escapism – you can bet that it represents the very best that the genre has to offer.

Whatever you like to read – trust Penguin.